CHRISTOPHER BUSH
THE CASE OF THE JUMBO SANDWICH

CHRISTOPHER BUSH was born Charlie Christmas Bush in Norfolk in 1885. His father was a farm labourer and his mother a milliner. In the early years of his childhood he lived with his aunt and uncle in London before returning to Norfolk aged seven, later winning a scholarship to Thetford Grammar School.

As an adult, Bush worked as a schoolmaster for 27 years, pausing only to fight in World War One, until retiring aged 46 in 1931 to be a full-time novelist. His first novel featuring the eccentric Ludovic Travers was published in 1926, and was followed by 62 additional Travers mysteries. These are all to be republished by Dean Street Press.

Christopher Bush fought again in World War Two, and was elected a member of the prestigious Detection Club.

He died in 1973.

CHRISTOPHER BUSH

THE CASE OF THE JUMBO SANDWICH

With an introduction
by Curtis Evans

DEAN STREET PRESS

INTRODUCTION

Rosalind. If it be true that good wine needs no bush [i.e., advertising], 'tis true that a good play needs no epilogue. Yet to good wine, they do use good bushes, and good plays prove the better by the help of good epilogues.

—SHAKESPEARE, Epilogue, *As You Like It*

THE decade of the 1960s saw the sun finally begin to set on that storied generation which between the First and Second World Wars gave us detective fiction's Golden Age. Taking account of both deaths and retirements, by the late Sixties only a bare half-dozen pre-World War Two members of the Detection Club were still plying their deliciously deceptive craft: Agatha Christie, Anthony Gilbert (Lucy Beatrice Malleson), Gladys Mitchell, John Dickson Carr, Nicholas Blake and Christopher Bush, the subject of this introduction. Bush himself would pass away, at the age of eighty-seven, in 1973, having published, at the age of eighty-two, his sixty-third Ludovic Travers detective novel, *The Case of the Prodigal Daughter*, in the United Kingdom in the spring of 1968.

In the United States Bush's final detective novel did not appear until late November 1969, about four months after the horrific Manson murders in the tarnished Golden State of California. Implicating the triple terrors of sex, drugs and rock and roll (not to mention almost inconceivably bestial violence), the Manson slayings could not have strayed farther from the whimsically escapist "death as a game" aesthetic of Golden Age of detective fiction. Increasingly in the decade capable of producing psychedelic psychopaths like Charles Manson and his "family," the few remaining survivors of the Golden Age of detective fiction increasingly deemed themselves men and women far out of time. In his detective fiction John Dickson Carr, an incurable romantic, prudently beat a retreat from the present into the pleasanter pages of the past, setting his tales in bygone historical eras where he felt vastly more at home. With varying success Agatha Christie made a brave effort to stay abreast of the times (*Third Girl, Endless Night*), but ultimately her strivings to understand what was going on around her collapsed into the utter incoherence of *Passenger to Frankfurt* and *Postern of Fate*, by general consensus the worst mystery novels that Dame Agatha ever put down on paper.

In his detective fiction Christopher Bush, who was not quite two years older than Christie, managed rather better than the Queen of Crime to keep up with all the unsettling goings-on around him, while never forswearing the Golden Age article of faith that the primary purpose of a crime writer is pleasingly to puzzle his/her readers. And, in contrast with Christie and Carr, Bush knew when it was time to lay down his pen (or turn off his dictation machine, as the case may be), thereby allowing him to make his exit from the stage on a comparatively high note. Indeed, Christopher Bush's concluding baker's dozen of detective novels, which he published between 1957 and 1968 (and which have now been reprinted, after more than a half-century, by Dean Street Press), makes a generally fine epilogue, or coda, to the author's impressive corpus of crime fiction, which first began to see the light of day way back in the jubilant Jazz Age. These are, readers will find, "good bushes" (to punningly borrow from Shakespeare), providing them with ample intelligent detective entertainment as Bush's longtime series sleuth Ludovic Travers, in the luminous twilight of his career, makes his final forays into ingenious criminal investigation.

*

In the last thirteen Ludovic Travers mystery novels, Travers' *entrée* to his cases continues to come through his ownership of the Broad Street Detective Agency. Besides Travers we also regularly encounter his elegant wife, Bernice (although sometimes his independent-minded spouse is away on excursions of her own), his proverbially loyal secretary, Bertha Munney, his top Broad Street op, Hallows (another one named French, presumably inspired by Bush's late Detection Club colleague Freeman Wills Crofts, pops up occasionally), John Hill of the United Assurance Agency, who brings Travers many of his cases, and Scotland Yard's Inspector Jewle and Sergeant Matthews, who after the first of these final novels, *The Case of the Treble Twist* (in the U.S. *Triple Twist*), are promoted, respectively, to Superintendent and Inspector. (The Yard's ex-Superintendent George Wharton, now firmly retired from any form of investigative work whatsoever, is mentioned just once by Ludo, when, in *The Case of the Dead Man Gone,* he passingly imparts that he and Wharton recently had lunch together.)

For all practical purposes Travers, who during the Golden Age was a classic gentleman amateur snooper like Philo Vance and Lord Peter Wimsey, now functions fully as a professional private eye—although one, to be sure, who is rather posher than the rest. While some reviewers referred to Travers as England's Philip Marlowe, in fact he little resembles the general run of love and leave 'em/hate and beat 'em brand of brutish American P.I.'s, favoring a nice cup of coffee (a post-war change from tea), a good pipe and the occasional spot of sherry to the frequent snatches of liquor and cigarettes favored by most of his American brethren and remaining faithful to his spouse despite encountering a succession of sexy women, not all of them, shall we say, virtuously inclined.

This was a formula which throughout the period maintained a devoted audience on both sides of the Atlantic consisting, one surmises, of readers (including crime writers Anthony Berkeley, Nicholas Blake and the late Alan Hunter, creator of Inspector George Gently) who preferred their detectives something less than hard-boiled. Travers himself sneers at the hugely popular (and psychotically violent) postwar American private eye Mike Hammer, commenting of an American couple in *The Case of the Treble Twist*: "She was a woman of considerable culture; his ran about as far as Mickey Spillane" [a withering reference to Mike Hammer's creator]. Yet despite his manifest disdain for Mike Hammer, an ugly American if ever there were one, Christopher Bush and his wife Florence in the spring of 1957 had traveled to New York aboard the RMS *Queen Elizabeth*, and references by him to both the United States and Canada became more frequent in the books which followed this trip.

Certainly *The Case of the Treble Twist* (1957) features tough customers and an exceptionally cruel murder, yet it is also one of Bush's most ingeniously contrived cases from the Fifties, full of charm, treacherous deception and, yes, plenty of twists, including one that is a real sockaroo (to borrow, as Bush occasionally did, from American idiom). Similarly clever is *The Case of the Running Man* (1958), which draws, as several earlier Bush books had, on the author's profound love and knowledge of antiques. By this time Bush and his wife, their coffers having burgeoned from the proceeds of his successful mysteries, resided in the quaint medieval market town of Lavenham, Suffolk at the Great House, a splendidly decorated fourteenth-century structure with an elegant Georgian-era façade which he and Florence purchased in 1953 and resided in until their deaths. The dashing author, whom in 1967 *Chicago Tribune* mystery reviewer Alice Crombie swooningly dubbed "one of the handsomest mystery writers on either side of the Channel or Atlantic," also drove a Jaguar, beloved by James Bond films of late, well into his eighties.

The Case of the Running Man includes that Golden Age detective fiction staple, a family tree, but more originally the novel features as a major character a black American man, Sam, the devoted chauffeur of the wealthy murder victim. Sam, who reminds Ludovic Travers of Rochester, "Jack Benny's factotum of television and radio," is an interesting and sincerely treated individual, although as Anthony Boucher amusingly pronounced at the time in the *New York Times Book Review*, he speaks "a dialect never heard by mortal ear"—an odd compounding of "American Negro" and London cockney.

The Case of the Careless Thief (1959) takes Ludo to Sandbeach, "the Blackpool of the South Coast," as the American jacket blurb puts it, with "a dozen hotels, a race track, a dog track, a music hall and two enormous dance halls." Anthony Boucher deemed this hard-hitting, tricky tale, which draws to strong effect on contemporary events in England, "one of Ludovic Travers' best cases." Likewise hard-hitting are *The Case of the Sapphire Brooch* (1960) and *The Case of the Extra Grave* (1961), complex tales of murderous mésalliances with memorably grim conclusions. The plot of *The Case of the Dead Man Gone*

(1961) topically involves refugee relief groups, while *The Case of the Heavenly Twin* (1963) opens with a case of a creative criminal couple forging American Express Travelers Checks, concerning which Americans of a certain age will recall actor Karl Malden sternly enjoining, in a long-running television advertising campaign: "Don't leave home without them." In contrast with many of his crime writing contemporaries (judging from the tone of their work), Bush actually learned to watch and enjoy television, although in *The Case of The Three-Ring Puzzle*, a tale of violently escalating intrigue, Travers dryly references Scottish philosopher Thomas Carlyle's famous observation that England's population consisted of "mostly fools" when he comments: "I guess he wasn't too far out at that. But rather remarkable an estimate perhaps, considering that in his day there were no television commercials."

Of Bush's final five Ludovic Travers detective novels, published between 1964 and 1968, when the Western World, in the eyes of many, was going from whimsically mod to utterly mad, the best are, in my estimation, the cases of *The Jumbo Sandwich* (1965), *The Good Employer* (1966) and *The Prodigal Daughter* (1968). In *Sandwich* a crisp case of a defrauded (and jilted) gentry lady friend of Ludo's metamorphoses into a smorgasbord of, as the American book jacket puts it, "blackmail, black magic, a black sheep, and murder." It all culminates in a confrontation on a lonely Riviera beach in France, setting of some of Ludovic Travers' earliest cases, between Ludo and a desperate killer, in which Bernice plays an unexpectedly active part. Ludo again travels to France in the highly classic *Employer*, which draws most engagingly on the sleuth's (and the author's) dabbling in the world of art and is dedicated to his distinguished Lavenham artist friends, the couple Reginald and Rosalie Brill, who resided next door to Bush and his wife at the fourteenth-century Little Hall, then an art student hostel for which the Brills served as guardians. In *The Guardian* Francis Iles (aka Golden Age crime writer Anthony Berkeley) pronounced that *Employer* represented Bush "at his most ingenious."

Finally, in *Daughter* Travers finds himself tasked with recovering the absconded teenage offspring of domineering Dora Marport, sober-sided head of the organization Home and Family, which is righteously devoted to "the fostering, so to speak, of family life as the stoutest bulwark against the encroachment of ever-more numerous hostile forces: sex and violence in literature, films and on television; pornography generally, and the erosion of responsibility and the capability for sacrifice by the welfare state." Can Travers, a Great War veteran who made his debut in detective fiction in 1926, bridge the generation gap in late-Sixties London? Ludo may prefer Bach to the Beatles, but in this, the last of his recorded cases, he proves more "with it" than one might have expected. All in all, *Daughter* makes a rewarding finish to one of the longest-running and most noteworthy sleuth series in British detective fiction.

Curtis Evans

PART I

1
BUYING A HORSE

IT WAS quite a few years since I'd seen Isabel Herne, and if I'd been told that morning when I arrived as usual at the Broad Street Detective Agency that she was going to call on me professionally, I'd have been—as Pepys would have put it—mightily surprised. When Bertha, our secretary-receptionist, put her call through to me, it took me a second or two to realise who it was at the other end of the line. I had to talk in circles till I'd placed her and even then I had to do some quick thinking.

"Of course I'll be delighted to see you," I told her. "You're staying in town?"

"No, I came up specially to see you. Only just arrived. I'm actually ringing from Charing Cross Station."

She said she'd like to see me straight away, so I told her to take a taxi. That gave me a minimum of ten minutes in which to think things over. I reached for a pad and jotted down an executive word or two—Holtacre, Sir George, Lady Herne, Isabel and the pony. Holtacre, that lovely place of theirs under the Sussex Downs: Sir George, killed in the hunting field—when was it?—some six or seven years back. The Hernes didn't often come to town, but she was a very distant relation of my wife and Sir George was a member of my club. My one visit to Holtacre was paid about a couple of years before his death, but I remembered Isabel, grown well beyond childhood, schooling a pony for a friend. Then I knew there was something else I ought to remember so I buzzed through to Bertha.

"About coffee, Bertha. Bring in two cups when Miss Herne arrives, and get me Mrs. Travers."

It was just after half-past ten and I was lucky to find Bernice at home.

"Lady Herne died about two years ago," she told me. "Don't you remember my writing Isabel a letter of condolence?"

"So you did," I said. "Isabel's coming to see me in a few minutes on business, heaven knows why. Anything else I ought to know about the family?"

"Not that I remember. I seem to think Holtacre has been let or sold. Isabel isn't married as far as I know."

"She isn't," I said. "At least, she introduced herself as Isabel Herne. How old is she now?"

"About twenty-seven. No, a bit older. She came of age just before her father was killed. You think she'd like to have lunch with us somewhere?"

I said she might be staying in town, so there'd be ample time to arrange a friendly meal. Then I had another look at my headlines and did some more thinking. The call would definitely be not a social one and, if it had brought her specially to town, then it was useless to try to think of reasons. All the same, I couldn't help wondering just what a wealthy young woman like Isabel Herne could be wanting with a detective agency. I knew she was wealthy. I knew that her father had settled a considerable sum on her just before he died and, in addition, there'd be the mother's estate—after death duties.

That was about all the speculation I had time for. Bertha was announcing the arrival. I had my door open and my best smile ready.

"Well, well, young lady. How nice to see you! Quite a few years since we met."

"I know," she said. "Time simply flies. And how are you both?"

"Bernice keeps remarkably well. I'm still managing to stay upright. In the geometrical sense, of course—not the spiritual."

The joke died at birth. I don't think she really heard me. Everything about her said there was something pretty serious on her mind. She did say she'd love some coffee. It was a chilly day of late autumn, but the room was warm and I helped her off with the heavy tweed coat and got her comfortably seated. She smelt awfully good, if I may put it that way. Some might have called it the smell of money, with the Chanel, Arpège or what-have-you merely an accessory. She was tall and, to my mind, beautifully dressed. The long, thinnish face had a tanned, outdoor look. Until she smiled she was almost freakishly plain, but to me it was in some curious way an attractive face. There was something friendly about it. It belonged to someone you'd instinctively trust.

"You're still living at the house?"

"Oh, no," she said, and still a bit nervously. "I leased it to some wealthy Americans. Very nice people who just love hunting. I'm at the Lodge. Quite large enough for me. And there're a couple of loose boxes."

"You still hunt?"

"But, of course! And I do quite a lot of work with the local pony clubs."

Coffee came in. She smiled a thanks to Bertha, took a sip and said it was good. And while I was wondering how to insinuate into the small talk the object of her visit, she suddenly put down the cup.

"About why I'm here. Of course I'm glad to see you again, if you know what I mean, but why I really came was—well, because you're you."

I smiled. "Wait a minute. Just what does that mean?"

"Well, you're a friend as well as being a detective." There was something almost aggressive about the plain statement. "I mean you're not the sort of person one reads about or sees on television. I don't have to worry about trusting you."

"You wouldn't in any case," I told her. "No agency could stay in business if it weren't trustworthy. In any case, just tell me in your own way and time exactly what it is that's worrying you."

"Well," she said, and still a bit defiantly, "it's about some money." She flushed slightly. "And about a man. I'd like you to try to recover the money, though it's not all that important, but I do want you to find the man and see he gets suitably punished."

"I see." I reached for the pad. "Start at the very beginning and tell me the whole story. Don't be afraid of being long-winded. Far better to put too much in than to leave something out. You never know what's important and what isn't."

She was frowning slightly as she finished her coffee and set the cup down.

"It's not going to be easy. I mean, having to admit one's been dreadfully stupid."

I smiled.

"I'm about old enough to be your father but still fool enough to make the most appalling mistakes. One day I'll make one and find I'm too old to recover from it. But you! At your age a mistake oughtn't to be much more than a triviality."

"Perhaps," she said. "It depends on the size of the mistake. And even at my age you can't brush things off all that easily."

This was how her story began. Horses had always been the main interest in life and then, a few weeks ago when she was at a race meeting with a couple of friends, she'd had what seemed at the time a marvellous revelation: she suddenly decided to own a racehorse herself: a real racehorse and not just a good point-to-point hunter. The idea must have been deep down for quite a time and only needed the occasion to break surface.

"I knew it was what I'd always wanted to do," she said. "It would give me a new interest in life and, after all, I could afford it, so there was no reason whatever why I shouldn't do it. It was rather odd, as it turned out, because the big Newmarket sales were due in only a few days, so what I did was book a room in Cambridge for the week. Every hotel at Newmarket would have been full up."

"You were alone?"

Her face reddened again. "Of course."

"Don't mistake me," I said hastily. "I wondered if you had a racing friend or possible trainer with you to give you advice."

She looked rather surprised. "I didn't think you'd know anything about racing."

I laughed. "Never underestimate the apparently ignorant. The fact is that when I was a boy, my father knew the owner of a large training establishment near our place in Suffolk, and one day I was taken round. It made a great impression on me and it's given me an interest ever since. I never back horses but I do take an interest. It's a relaxation, like crossword puzzles."

She actually smiled. "I suppose when it comes to it, I don't know an enormous deal myself, but I did want to handle the whole thing alone. That would be half the fun."

"You stagger me," I said. "Those sales are an event. Breeders and buyers and government agents from all over the world, let alone the trainers and heaven knows who. If it'd been me, I'd have been terrified."

"That's because you wouldn't know badly enough that you wanted to do it," she told me. "I intended to buy a horse at what I thought the right price and then get me a trainer; if possible, someone not too far from me in Sussex. Also, I wanted a filly rather than a colt in case I might be lucky enough to win a race or two with her and then be able to breed from her. That's why I booked the accommodation at Cambridge and that's where I met this man."

The flush was even more pronounced, and just for a moment she hesitated. "He called himself Edward Gower."

"Just a moment. Why the doubt? Have you already made some enquiries?"

"No," she said. "You're the only one I've spoken to. But I think you'll see. Shall I go on?"

The man made her acquaintance after dinner on the very first night at the hotel. He was about thirty, charmingly mannered and generally most attractive. Also he seemed to know an enormous deal about racing. His father was a baronet—Sir Mortimer Gower—who raced quite a lot up north. The following night he disclosed that he'd be attending the sales where he hoped to buy a horse himself. So there they were. Two people with the same interests and suddenly attracted to each other.

It was obvious from what she told me that he took charge from then on. There was advice and warnings; never, for instance, trust apparent bargains. Only rarely did a cheap horse turn out to be a gold mine. It was money that talked. He was buying his own horse more or less surreptitiously, he said, and it wouldn't be sent to his father's trainer. And then the two miraculously found something else in common. He, too, would prefer a filly to a colt, provided she had the kind of conformation that promised a future, top-class jumper. It was a kind of insurance. Many a horse mediocre on the flat had turned out to be a champion over the sticks. In any case, out of all the cosy chatting and planning and daydreaming, a decision was come to. A filly should, if possible, be bought: in his name, but in double ownership.

I broke in. "Let me ask you a very personal question, Isabel. Did he at any time give you the idea that he was wanting to be more than a friend?"

It was a hard question, and she didn't look at me. "He professed to find me very attractive."

"Nothing more? As the week progressed? That agreement, for example, on a partnership in the horse?"

"Perhaps, yes," she said, and she said it very quietly. "I know now I was an awful fool, but I really thought that once everything was settled in Newmarket he was going to propose to me. It was already arranged I was to go to Yorkshire to meet his people."

"I see. And the horse. One was actually bought?"

One was, at least ostensibly. There'd been no need to be precipitate and jump at any chance, so nothing happened till the Thursday, and then a certain filly seemed ideal. She'd been led out at six thousand guineas, having failed to reach her reserve. Edward Gower got to work behind the scenes. By that same evening he had valuable private information that made the filly cheap. On the Friday morning at Cambridge, he was able to announce he had a forty-eight-hour option at seven thousand guineas.

What happened then wasn't too hard to foresee. She handed over her cheque for half the amount and on the Sunday evening he left the hotel for Newmarket, where he'd stay till everything was completed. He rang her on the Monday night to say everything had gone off well and he was stabling the filly till the question of a trainer was settled. She still wanted a Sussex trainer and he agreed to get in touch with a likely one or two by telephone. When she expressed a wish to drive over and see the filly he said he'd arrange it for the Wednesday morning and confirm beforehand.

By lunchtime on the Wednesday nothing had happened, and at tea-time she rang the hotel where he was supposed to have stayed. No one of his name had been there. The next day she discovered that her cheque had been cashed. Through a friend enquiries were made at Tattersalls and she learned that the filly had been sold privately to an American buyer on the Friday. No one of the name of Edward Gower had been concerned in that sale.

"Tough luck," I told her quietly. "He was a slick operator. His sort have taken in far cleverer people than you or me."

"It was horrible," she said. "It nauseates me every time I think of it. It wasn't the money—believe me; it was all those calculated lies. And the treachery. I hope I'm not vindictive but I want to be in court when they sentence him."

"But not as a witness."

"No, no. Not that. That's why I never dreamt of going to the police. I'd hate people to know what a fool I'd been. But hasn't that sort of person what's known as a record? Previous convictions and that sort of thing?"

"Maybe," I said. "But let's be strictly logical. Imagine he's in court. On what charge? Previous convictions don't affect the matter; if he's in court it's on a wholly new charge. And who brings the charge? If you refuse to, then we can only assume that some time in the future he's going to swindle someone else and it's that someone else who's going to bring a charge. That reduces the whole thing to this. You wouldn't bring a charge now and therefore you're prepared to wait till some indefinite future when he's caught."

She'd been shifting uneasily in her chair. I leaned forward across the desk. "Isabel, don't let this business go on preying on your mind. Get it over with. Let me go along with you and report the whole thing to a friend of mine. The police will be most discreet; I promise you that."

She shook her head. "No. Not now. If you find him, perhaps I'll change my mind."

"You're the client," I told her. "I'm here to do what I can. But I've still got to protect your interests: I mean to point out difficulties and show what's involved. *Find the man*," I said. "Sounds simple enough till you think it over. He's got your money in his pocket and there isn't a place in the world he couldn't have gone to. I shall probably ask for a description of him, but even that isn't going to be all the help you'd think. Unless he's either cocksure or careless, he's by now changed his appearance so that his own mother wouldn't recognise him. You do see that, don't you?"

"Well—yes."

I tried an avuncular smile. "Then that's that. You're here for advice and you're going to get it. But you're not just an ordinary client. If an ordinary client had been told what I've just pointed out to you and he still insisted that I find his man, I wouldn't hesitate. That's why we're in business. So long as he paid, I'd go on hunting. But I can't let you do that. It would cost you an awful lot of money and with no assured results. So what I propose is this. Give me a fortnight and no longer. Every possible means will be used to unearth this swindler and for that you'll pay a flat sum of a hundred and fifty pounds. Also I promise you that even after we've officially ceased to be client and agent, we'll still go on keeping our ears to the ground and you'll be notified at once if we think things should be reopened. How's that?" I'd expected the same argumentative obstinacy but she actually smiled.

"I think that's very generous. Perhaps I've been a bit foolish. I mean, after what you've told me."

"That's fine," I said. "We'll do our best, always keeping in mind the fact that your name is on no account to be mentioned. Agreed?"

"Of course."

"Right. So let's start off with his description. You're sure he was English?"

"Absolutely sure."

"No trace of a foreign accent? No false intonations? Nothing unusual about his vocabulary?"

"No. He spoke perfect English. He told me he'd been to Harrow and I never had any doubt that he was telling the truth."

So to his description: about five-feet-ten and athletically built: black hair and neat, black moustache: nose slightly aquiline, eyes a greenish hazel. No visible skin blemishes or tattooing.

"Now about the possibility of finger-prints," I said. "Have you anything he handled? Any present he might have given you, for instance?"

"No. Nothing."

"What about his car?"

She frowned slightly. "Well, I never actually saw it. He said it was a Bentley and he'd been involved in an accident near Cambridge and had brought the car in for repairs. That was why he was actually at Cambridge waiting for the repairs to be finished. He'd intended originally to stay at Newmarket. We actually used my car."

"I see. And what about his clothes. Was he well-dressed?"

"Very well-dressed. Not obtrusive, if you know what I mean, but just how you'd expect anyone like him to be dressed."

"Jewellery?"

"Oh, no. Only a wrist-watch, if you can call that jewellery, and I think it was stainless steel."

"Did he smoke?"

"Only an occasional cigarette."

That seemed to be virtually all. Just one other thing, perhaps. "You've had quite a time to think things over, so do you recall anything that struck you at the time as being unusual or odd? Anything, say, that was the least bit out of keeping?"

She frowned as she tried to think back. "Sorry. I can't think of anything."

"Right," I said. "I'll have my secretary in and dictate an agreement. Stop me if there's anything you disagree with or wish altered."

There was just one thing you should know and that was what she said when I came to the hundred and fifty pounds fee.

"I think you should have a share of any of the money you recover. I think you ought to have at least a half."

That sort of optimism was out of this world. I didn't tell her so. I admitted that we usually had a bonus of ten per cent on recovered property and, if she wished, a clause to that effect could be inserted. She wished.

Bertha went out to type the two copies.

"While we're waiting, I'm going to try to do something," I told Isabel. "Has it possibly occurred to you that Edward Gower might have been the real name of that young man? That he might be the black sheep of his family?"

She stared. "But surely . . ."

"Plenty of crooks among the upper classes. Crime, you know, isn't the peculiar perquisite of the under-privileged. So suppose we try to find out?"

Debrett was handy enough on the reference shelf. I consulted the index for baronetcies and in less than no time found the Gowers. Theirs was George the Second, reasonably modern as some baronetcies go. The seat was Wormsley House, near Doncaster. I worked out Sir Mortimer's age as sixty-eight. His wife had died in 1961. There were three children of the marriage—two daughters and the son, Edward.

I called Bertha, gave her the necessary details and asked her to get me Wormsley House. I had another look at the entries for Edward. Harrow and Balliol. Just thirty and unmarried.

I lighted a cigarette for Isabel and stoked my pipe. Now that something was actually being done she was much more composed. And another thing I knew. For days she'd been living on her nerves, and now already the hour she'd spent in my office had had about it something highly therapeutic. I smiled to myself. Ludovic Travers, the old psycho-therapist, arch-soother and friend.

Bertha rang through with Wormsley House on the line. I picked up the receiver.

"Hallo. To whom am I speaking?"

"This is Ruth Gower," said a quite charming voice. "Who are you?"

"Travers, Miss Gower. Ludovic Travers. I run quite an important detective agency in Broad Street, London. That's where I'm speaking from. If you care to ring off now and call New Scotland Yard, I'm sure they'll be prepared to give you my credentials."

"I don't think that should be necessary. But a detective agency! Why should you be ringing me?"

"Not necessarily you, Miss Gower. Anybody who could give me information about your brother."

"Edward? I don't understand."

"This is the reason, Miss Gower. In the course of an investigation we've run across a man, who hasn't as yet been apprehended, who's been using your brother's name. Impersonation for the purpose of fraud."

"But this is dreadful! When did all this happen?"

"Within the last fortnight. I really rang you with the hope of warning your brother. You think I could speak with him?"

"I'm afraid not," she said. "He's a member of that Oxford Exploration Group that's now in New Guinea. He left about a month ago, and we don't expect him back for at least four months."

I thanked her. I was sure there'd be no repercussions affecting the family.

"Just one other question. Will you listen to this description of the man? He's about your brother's age, by the way, and claimed also to have been at Harrow."

She was just as bewildered as before. To her knowledge her brother had no such friend. Certainly no one of that description had ever been his guest at Wormsley House.

"I'm most grateful," I told her. "And please do ring New Scotland Yard if only to be assured this wasn't some kind of hoax. Also, if there should be any developments which might affect any of you, I'll inform you at once."

Isabel had been listening on the extension. She was looking a bit perplexed.

"Well, that clears that much up," I said. "Your man was definitely an impersonator. What we call clearing away the dead wood."

More talk would have done her no good. I helped her on with her coat and took her arm as we went through to Bertha's room. We signed the agreements and I went with her to the street.

"Feeling better?"

She smiled. "Much better. You've been more than good."

"Not a bit of it. You're staying in town, by the way?"

"Oh, no. I'm taking the first train back."

A taxi hove in sight and I hailed it. I was giving a rather sad shake of the head as it carried her out of sight.

2
EXPLORATION

I LIGHTED my pipe again, drew the client's chair nearer the fire and stretched my long legs towards the warmth. Somehow I'd never known such a curious morning. Everything about it was wholly beyond experience.

Arrogance of any sort is a deadly sin and the intellectual variety is far from excluded: all the same I couldn't help shaking my head again over Isabel Herne. There was even something pathetic about her and the confidence she'd had in her ability to handle a situation which, given even the same circumstances, I'd have been scared of handling myself. And there'd been that romantic business. With her utter lack of good looks she must have long since given up hopes of marriage and then suddenly, as from a stage trap-door, up had popped a Prince Charming. She hadn't been a piano on which he'd been able to play. She'd been a pianola, and all he'd had to do was touch a switch. It had been as easy as that. The scent of her was still in the room, and somehow everything was still a highly personal matter. I've run up against quite a number of con-men and general swindlers in my time and I hate their slimy furtiveness. I hate all spielers, whether they're men like the fake Gower or merely posers as doctors, dentists, men of affairs or ordinary housewives who reel off their patter in television commercials. I hate the half-truths which are worse than lies.

I wanted to find Edward Gower—I'll go on calling him that to avoid confusion—and I wanted to see him in the dock, but to say that I had hopes would have been in itself a super-optimism. The only chance was that he might have a record.

Ideas suddenly began to coalesce as I leaned back in the comfortable chair, and all at once I was virtually sure that Gower had no record. The more I thought about him, the more I was sure he was not a pro but a lucky amateur. Consider, for instance, what might have happened if he'd played his cards otherwise. He could just have gone along with her in that business of buying a horse, gone on making love to her and finally married her. A fortune and not a comparatively measly three-thousand five-hundred guineas.

The real pro takes time to think things over, and not till he's ready does he make any real move. Gower hadn't planned. He'd spun his lies at once and so spoiled his chance of a wealthy marriage. The pro's relatives would either have been non-existent, that is to say, all dead, or living at the other ends of the earth. And another thing. Con-men are very rarely lone wolves. A confederate is an essential to bolster up claims and status.

As I saw it, Gower had had to extemporise. Once he'd learned about her intention to buy a filly, he'd known somehow there was money in it for himself. He'd had no real plan but he'd certainly had the ability to seize upon the possibilities in the sudden chance that presented itself. Even then he could never have succeeded but for the amazing credulity of Isabel herself. It made me wince when I saw the couple in my mind's eye: roseate day after day on that stand above the sale ring as this horse and that was led round; sharing excitements over bids: he quietly affectionate and she all starry-eyed.

I glanced at my watch as I came to a sudden decision. It was almost half-past twelve, and I hoped to get Jewle at the Yard. I'd seen him only two days before. Now he happened to be in. I asked if he'd had lunch and he hadn't. I said I'd stand him one at our usual restaurant near Westminster Bridge. He said he'd book a table for one o'clock.

I apologise if you've heard all this before, but Jewle— Detective-Superintendent Jewle—is a very old friend. I've actually worked with him and we've been friends for quite twenty years and that's a pretty long time. He's tall—though short of my six-three—heavily built, dark, quiet in manner and even more reliable than they usually come. We've long since ceased to work together, but if he can lend us at Broad Street a legitimate hand, he does. If we run across anything in which he might be interested, we pass it on.

He knew very well I hadn't so suddenly asked him out to lunch for mere friendship's sake but he asked no questions. It was not till we'd settled in on the main course that I began the story. There was nothing surreptitious about it. All I had to do to keep within the terms of the agreement was not to divulge my client's name. I knew what his first reactions would be. Why hadn't she gone to the police? The local police, and valuable time not wasted. I told him I'd begged her to go to the police. I'd even offered to accompany her.

"It's the old story," I said. "You and I know the best friend a con-man or blackmailer has is the fear of publicity. My idea is, though, that if he can be located I can induce her to bring the charge."

"Yes," he said, and went on with his meal. But I could see he was interested.

"A curious case," he said in a moment or two. "A whole lot of curious things about it. That particular kind of swindle for instance. It's a wholly new one on me."

You can get an enormous deal from an argument so I kept the ball rolling. I put up that theory of mine about Gower's being an amateur.

"I think you're right," he said. "Looks to me as if he was on the run from something or other, and then this chance dropped right in his lap. But why did he choose the name of a real person?"

I told him I thought I could explain it. That New Guinea expedition had been quite well publicized. I'd seen something about it on television. Gower had seen it and had taken advantage of the fact that the man whose name he could use would be safely out of England for quite a time.

"Might be," he said. "But this client of yours. You think her description was reliable?"

"Sure of it," I said. "She was expensively educated and moves only in the best circles. If she described Gower as someone of her own class, then I'd say he was. She'd have noticed any aberrations. When you add that to his personal description, your people might be able to turn something up."

"Well, I'll see what we can do," he told me. "Anything else?"

"Only this. I can't afford to leave anything unchecked so I'll see if he did have a car at a Cambridge garage. I also might go on to Newmarket and see if I can pick up anything there. If you like to ring the Cambridge police and ask them to lend a hand, I'll be grateful."

"See what I can do," he said. "When are you going?"

Not till early the next morning, I said, so he'd give me a ring in the early evening. He hadn't time for coffee so I paid the bill and walked across with him to North-umberland Avenue. In Duncannon Street I took a bus.

The first thing I did when I got back was to ring the Chaucer Hotel at Cambridge. Luckily I was able to book a room for the following night. I said I'd be in to lunch. I got on with the work that Isabel's call had interrupted, and it was just after five o'clock when Jewle rang.

"We think we've got a connection with your man," he told me. "I'll take it slowly if you want to write it down."

Six weeks previously a man answering to the Edward Gower description and calling himself Major Guy Abbott had stayed for almost a week at a Winchester hotel and had left without paying his bill. Property and cash of a value of about a hundred pounds were missing from a guest's room. A fortnight later a man of the same description, but calling himself Dr. Charles Prince, disappeared after a stay of four days at a Bournemouth hotel and with him went the proceeds of thefts from two of the hotel rooms: cash about two hundred pounds and jewellery roughly valued at five hundred.

"One interesting fact," Jewle said, "is that there's a television room at that last hotel, and the B.B.C. televised a preview of that New Guinea expedition while he was actually there. Hence the Edward Gower name as you suggested. Oh, and one other thing. The hair's not to be relied on. At Winchester it was dark but at Bournemouth it was a light brown, almost blond. No moustache in either case."

He'd also rung Cambridge for me. I was to ask for a Detective-Inspector Brownwell.

Just as I thanked him I thought of something. "Any finger-prints in those two hotel cases?"

"Yes," he said. "We were lucky to get them in both. That's how the two got tied in. The unusual thing is that there were no previous records either here or with Interpol. Winchester seems to have been the start of what's becoming a lucrative career. Wonder what he'll branch off into next."

I wondered too. Then, too late to put it up to Jewle, I wondered something else. Had that career begun six weeks ago because our man had only then arrived in England? Could he, for instance, have arrived at Southampton and gone the few miles to Winchester? And later doubled back, as it were, to Bournemouth? Naturally I didn't know it, but it definitely seemed a likelihood. Whether it could be made use of was far more problematical.

But there was a line of enquiry which could be followed at once, and I ought to have thought of it while Isabel was in the office. Luckily for me she was back at home. She said she'd just finished a belated tea.

"Something I ought to have remembered this morning," I said. "You said that cheque of yours had been cashed. I take it that you rang your local bank to enquire and they said the cheque had come through from the clearing house. Was it endorsed?"

I had to wait while she found the actual cheque. It hadn't been endorsed.

"Then the so-called Edward Gower paid it into an account of his own somewhere. Do you know where?"

She was a far better business-woman than I'd thought. The cheque had been paid in at a certain Newmarket bank.

"Good," I said. "I'll be making discreet enquiries there. By the way, I've some good news for you. He's wanted by the police on two other charges, so you needn't worry about ever having to give evidence yourself."

Cambridge is not much over a fifty-mile trip. Once clear of the suburbs there was very little traffic, and it was still short of half-past ten when I contacted Brownwell. He was in his late forties; quiet spoken, obviously efficient and with the right knowledge of local conditions. We got along just fine.

We had coffee in a near-by restaurant and I made him acquainted with the case. The only thing I left out was my client's name. He remembered seeing the Winchester and Bournemouth cases in the *Police Gazette* and said he could refresh his memory from his files.

"And you'd like us to trace a possible car."

"If you will," I said. "Mind you, I think it's a hundred to one against his ever having had a car, but you know as well as I do it's something we just can't neglect. Even if he did have a car, it's a thousand to one it wasn't a Bentley." He said he'd have every garage checked. He had my description of Gower and, if necessary, he could supplement it from the *Gazette*.

"Anything else? Anything I can do for you at Newmarket? I spent my first ten years there so I've a lot of connections." I wanted to handle that cheque business myself, so I put it to him that the actual scene of the swindle wasn't of any great importance. All the relative facts were known. It would have been folly for Gower to have really contacted any of the filly's connections. I'd already had to skate on some pretty thin ice when I'd had to tell him I'd be staying the night at the Chaucer. The last thing I wanted was for him to make enquiries there and so make a good guess at the identity of my client.

He left straight away. He'd contact me round about five and give me the results of his enquiries. I stayed on and had another cup of coffee. It was quite a time since I'd been in Cambridge, and I'd thought of looking up my old college. Now I was actually back I was realising that there's no search quite so futile and frustrating as that for a long-vanished youth.

I collected my car and drove to the hotel. It was small-ish—only forty rooms—but as nice a place as I'd run across for quite a time. The desk was courteous and friendly, the lounges were comfortable and the mattress in my quite large bedroom was as springy as a trampoline. There was even a socket for my electric razor. The dining-room was warm but airy, and the lunch itself first-class.

It's only a thirteen-mile drive to Newmarket, and at half-past two I was shown into the office of the manager of the bank. I showed him the agency's warrant card, referred him to Brownwell and Jewle and told him precisely why I was there. He wasn't all that surprised. There'd been at the time something unusual about that cheque withdrawal.

The customer—there was no doubt about his being our man—had been interviewed on the Thursday afternoon of sales week about opening an account. His credentials had seemed excellent and the account was duly opened with a hundred pounds in cash. Gower had therefore known as early as that that the swindle was as good as in the bag.

"He told me he was at Newmarket for the sales," the manager said, "and I did look him up later on in *Debrett*. The next time I saw him was on the Tuesday afternoon. We then had the cheque for 3,500 guineas which he'd paid in on the Friday. He said there'd been a change of plans. In the morning he was taking possession of a colt and the seller wanted payment in cash. Probably some income-tax swindle which was no concern of his, but he wanted to close his account early the next morning. He apologised for having given us so much trouble and said he naturally expected to be charged for it. He was most charming about it. As far as we were concerned, everything was in order and the account was closed soon after we opened the next morning."

"How was he paid?"

"Two thousand in five-pound notes and the rest in one pound."

"You have the numbers?"

He smiled.

"Afraid we haven't. This is a tremendously busy branch and we handle large sums, often in cash. By some of our standards, his transactions were very small indeed. As far as we're concerned, even now, there's been no fraud committed."

I agreed. I supposed he'd no idea of any further intentions on Gower's part and, except for what he'd already told me, he hadn't. I thanked him and left.

I had tea at the hotel, and read for a bit in the smoking-lounge waiting for Brownwell's call. It came just after five.

"Nothing doing at all." he said. "Every garage has been covered. Anything else I can do?"

I said that since Gower hadn't left by car, it was probably by rail. A bus would have been too conspicuous. As he was at Newmarket on the Wednesday morning, or so I'd gathered, there was just the chance to check where he'd gone. We agreed that if anything was unearthed, it should be reported direct to Jewle. I thanked him warmly for what he'd done, and told him to look me up when he was next in town.

I wasn't proposing to see the manager till well after dinner, when he'd almost certainly be free, and meanwhile I had best part of two hours to spend. As I sat on in that lounge I wasn't at all happy. I'd known even before I'd left town that morning that there'd be no car. With some of the proceeds of the Bournemouth thefts still available, he'd come to the comparative quiet of a Cambridge hotel with the hope of pulling off another job, and it was a hundred to one he'd arrived by train. As for that call on the bank manager, I'd known in my heart of hearts that the best it could bring was a verification of facts already known. In fact, I might just as well have stayed on in town myself.

I don't often get that feeling of futility, but now there was in it a certain *amour propre*. There was no pleasure in knowing that the police were looking for Edward Gower and that their chance of finding him, as compared with my own, was at least fifty to one on. Unreasonable of me, perhaps, but I'd taken on a job and I wanted to see it through myself. If Gower was caught, I wanted the Agency to have some credit for it, even if we didn't do the actual catching. The futility lay in the fact that at the moment I could see nothing ahead but other futilities. I could even get so far as telling myself that the sensible thing to do was to return to Isabel the balance of her fee and assure her that the police were tactfully taking over.

I went upstairs and had a bath, chiefly to pass the time. I was standing myself a drink in the bar when the gong went for dinner. It was another excellent meal. Wyatt, the manager, made the round of the tables as a good manager should, and we had a brief chat. He seemed quite pleased when I said mine would be a short but uncommonly pleasant stay and that next time I hoped to bring my wife.

I spent an hour in the television lounge, then a quick look in the dining-room showed it deserted. The desk called Wyatt for me on the house phone and I was told to come to the office. As I went in he was coming through a door on the right, which was evidently his private lounge. He gave me a smile.

"You wanted to see me, Mr. Travers?"

I said I'd be grateful if he could spare me a minute or two. Was he married? He was. I said it might be as well if his wife heard what I had to say. He disappeared for a moment or two, then came back with her; a short, buxom woman whom I'd seen before and taken for a guest. She gave me quite an anxious look.

"I'm not making complaints," I told them. "Quite the contrary. This is one of the very nicest hotels I've ever stayed at. But perhaps you'd better see this."

They had a look at the agency warrant card. Wyatt stared.

"You're a private detective?"

I broke it by degrees. I'd been working most of the day with the local police. Trying to trace a man who'd recently been one of their guests. A man calling himself Edward Gower.

"But that's incredible." That was Mrs. Wyatt. "He was such a charming man. He was obviously a gentleman."

"Part of the equipment," I said. "The real Edward Gower was thousands of miles away and he knew it. He's wanted for thefts while he was staying at hotels at Winchester and Bournemouth, and he was almost certainly here with another theft in mind. What I'm here to do is make sure he was really here for that purpose."

They still couldn't believe it. Nothing of the sort had ever happened at the Chaucer. It was almost lèse-majesté. And then she thought of something.

"That Miss Herne," she told her husband. "They used always to be together."

"Miss Herne is to be kept out of it," I said. "It was she who had suspicions about him and reported it to me, and I reported it to Scotland Yard. It seems this so-called Gower changed his mind about robbery in this hotel and tried to swindle her out of quite a large sum of money instead. At the very last she got suspicious."

"It's incredible," Wyatt said. "What do you want us to do?"

"Just answer a few questions. How did he contact you, for instance?"

"He rang. I'm almost sure he said he was ringing from London. That was on the Thursday and he wanted to come down the next day."

"How did he arrive?"

"I can't say. All I know is he came here by taxi."

"And he left on the evening of the following Sunday week. Did he pay his bill?"

"Most certainly. Both he and Miss Herne told me he was going to Newmarket on business. She was staying on for a day or two."

"I know," I said. "He was supposed to return a day or two later and pick her up here. Did he make any telephone calls during his stay?"

Wyatt consulted his records. There'd been no calls.

"And his room. I suppose it's been occupied since?"

"Oh, yes. The very next day."

I explained the question. To make absolutely sure that Gower was the Winchester and Bournemouth man—we had his fingerprints for both jobs—we wanted prints he might have left at the hotel.

"You've nothing personal of his that might have had prints on it."

There was nothing he could think of. His wife had a sudden idea. "What about that book?"

"What book?"

"You remember. The book Ada found in a drawer in his room."

"Oh, that," he said.

It was in a drawer of his desk, handy if the guest should remember it and ask for it to be sent on.

"Don't touch it," I told him quickly. "How many people have handled it, Mrs. Wyatt?"

Ada, the chambermaid, and herself, she said. Wyatt found a sheet of brown paper and I took the book from the drawer with just a finger and thumb at a corner. It was a virtually new Penguin edition of *Lady Chatterley's Lover*.

"Not a very nice book, so I believe."

"Depends on your tastes," I told him as I carefully wrapped it up. He found some Scotch tape to hold the wrapping down.

There were thanks all round. I assured them that they'd not be troubled again. If by any chance the local police called, Miss Herne's name was on no account to be mentioned. There'd definitely be no bad publicity for the hotel.

By nine the next morning I'd paid my bill. Wyatt saw me off and was almost effusive in his thanks. It was a fine morning and I could have made good time if I'd been in a hurry to get back to town. But I couldn't say I was happy: indeed, if the hotel hadn't been the kind of hotel it was, I might have been thoroughly disgruntled. The lucky chance of finding a book which would almost certainly have Gower's prints and so tie him in with the other two cases, didn't make me any happier. Quite the contrary.

All I could do was hand the book over to Jewle and leave the Yard to handle things, which meant that the only possible thing for me to do was to ring Isabel Herne, tell her guardedly what had happened and return her the balance of her cheque. Even if we threw into the hunt for Gower every man we could spare from other jobs, we had no better than a thousand to one chance of finding him. Well over a month had elapsed since that Bournemouth job, and even the police hadn't been able to pick him up. What chance, then, did we stand?

I got back to the office just short of eleven, had a word with Norris, our general manager, had Bertha ring my wife and then get me Jewle. I gave him a brief account of my trip and he told me to let him have the book as soon as I could. I said if it suited him I'd bring it along in the course of the next half-hour.

I took the book out of my bag and thought I'd have a look at it myself. I put on some gloves so as not to complicate the prints, undid the wrappings and flicked the pages over. That was when I saw the visiting card.

That, I guessed, would be one he'd had printed when he'd planned the descent on the Chaucer. I had a look at the back—I don't know why—and saw some faintly pencilled numbers. I had a look at them through the glass. COV 1028. It had to be a telephone number—Covent Garden 1028.

A moment or two and I was dialling the number. Another moment and a man's crisp voice. "Maylock's, Turf Accountants."

I don't know why I had the sense to act as quickly as I did.

"Sorry," I said, "wrong number."

3
ON THE TRAIL

JEWLE seemed delighted to have the book. His regular side-kick, Matthews, was there and he sent him out with it straight away.

"You'd like some coffee?"

I said I would. He rang for a couple of cups, then suggested I should tell him again about the Cambridge trip. I went over the whole thing in detail: indeed I'd actually finished my coffee by the time I'd reached the end.

"Not much there," he said. "Except, of course, the book."

"No need to worry about handling this," I said, and gave him the visiting card. "I found it in the book. Gower had used it to mark his place. Take a look at the back."

He looked. His hand fairly shot out towards the buzzer.

"No need to ring," I said. "I did it as soon as I found the card. It's the number of a firm of bookmakers. Maylock's. I rang off as soon as I found out. Said I'd called a wrong number."

"Maylock's," he said, and frowned. "That rings a faint bell. Bookmakers. Gower had had dealings with them?"

"Probably. Or was proposing to."

He thought for a moment. "Not proposing to. Almost certainly had. He disappeared after Bournemouth and he may have been telling the truth when he told the Chaucer he was ringing from London. Anything else do you make of it?"

"Only that in view of his racing knowledge—I mean as shown when he was working the swindle—he was the kind of person who might do a bit of betting."

Matthews came in then. Gower's prints were in the book. He was now definitely tied in with Winchester and Bournemouth.

"Better get something ready for the *Gazette*," Jewle told him. "Mr. Travers and I are going to pay a little call."

He checked the actual address of Maylock's and we left. At that time of morning Underground is quickest. To walk is the next best thing. We got off at Covent Garden and walked through the market outskirts and into the maze of streets behind. Maylock's was in Churston Street, the first floor of an antiquated building that called itself Churston House. There was a lift and we took it.

You could just have swung a cat in the enquiry room. A thinnish woman of about forty was at the desk.

"Any of the principals in?"

"There's only Mr. Bert," she said. "Mr. Fred died last year. What name, please?"

"Superintendent Jewle of New Scotland Yard."

She shot him a look as she reached for the receiver. A minute and she was telling us to go through.

Her other door opened on a large room partitioned off into a couple of smaller rooms. Half-a-dozen men with head-phones were seated at what might be called a long desk. On the opposite wall was an immense blackboard where a couple of men with erasers and chalk were marking up prices. An enormous electric clock with second hand was on the wall at the left.

A man was coming to meet us from a door in one of the partitions. He looked about sixty: tallish, spare and bald. He looked at me and then at Jewle. I must have puzzled him. No one looks less like a policeman. It was Jewle who held out a hand.

"Mr. Maylock?"

"That's right. Bert Maylock. Sorry I had to keep you waiting but I had to arrange for my assistant to take over. What can I do for you, Superintendent?"

He was just a bit nervous.

"Give us some information—we hope. Anywhere quiet we can talk?"

We went through a door in the other partition and into a medium-sized office. The desk had three telephones. The principal furnishings were filing cabinets, but there were enough chairs to go round. Jewle introduced me and we sat down. The voices from the main room only just filtered through.

"Not your busiest time," suggested Jewle.

"Just warming up," Maylock said. "And now what can I do for you gentlemen?"

Jewle smiled dryly. "We might want to open credit accounts, except that we don't. What we do want is a complete account of any dealings you had with a certain Edward Gower."

Maylock sat very still. He didn't speak for a moment.

"You know I can't do that, Superintendent. Even if we did have any such dealings, they were confidential. You can't do business like that."

"Come off it!" Jewle made it amusedly. "You know as well as I do that in less than no time I can get an order and impound all your books. You wouldn't want me to do that—not unless there'd been any hanky-panky."

"All right. But I resent that remark."

"Go on resenting," Jewle told him. "I'll apologise as soon as you tell me what I want to know."

Maylock simmered for a moment or two. "What was the name again?"

"Edward Gower," Jewle said patiently.

"Oh, yes. Edward Gower. Well, he came personally after giving us a ring and wanted to open a credit account. His father was a well-known northern owner but he didn't want him to know. Seems he had an objection to all forms of betting. At any rate I looked him over and he opened an account in the sum of a hundred and fifty pounds. I gave him a copy of our rules, and then I looked him up after he'd gone and everything seemed in order. Not that we worry too much about that. The best guarantee was having his money. He'd paid cash."

"What was his town address?"

"The Excelsior. Melbourne Place. He said he'd be staying there for at least a month."

"So far, so good. Tell us about his operations."

"Well, the first week he was up and down—"

"Just a minute," Jewle said. "You have an enormous lot of clients one way and another, so how do you happen to remember the transactions of just one? And without reference to your records?"

"You'll see in a minute," Maylock told him. "But about his bets. He was up and down, as I said. Then he had a bad week. The account was only about ten pounds in the black. Then he had quite a big bet: fifty each way at sevens. When it was passed to me I did some checking and had his hotel rung but he'd gone out. I let the bet stand and laid some of it off. The horse ran fourth of eleven, and when I got no answer after we'd sent in his account we rang his hotel again but he'd checked out."

"You didn't lose much?"

"Thirty quid. I didn't want to make any trouble so I wrote it off as a bad debt, and then what d'you think happened?"

"A few days ago he turned up full of apologies and paid up," I said.

He stared. "How'd you know?"

"I didn't. I was in a position to make a good guess."

"Well, you guessed right," he told me a bit grudgingly. "He said he'd been called away unexpectedly and the whole thing had slipped his mind."

"And then he opened a fresh account?"

"No, he said he was going home. Catching an afternoon train to Yorkshire. He said he'd just about enough for the ticket: after paying me, that is."

"And that's the last you saw or heard of him?"

"Absolutely the last."

Jewle did a little thinking. Maylock cut in. "Now do you mind, Superintendent, telling me what all this is about? In confidence, of course."

I thought Jewle would be telling him he'd had a very lucky escape, but he didn't.

"Just a bit of family trouble. Can't be more explicit than that. Nothing to do with betting. Between ourselves, he's wanted as a witness. Keep that strictly under your hat."

He got to his feet and held out his hand. "Sorry if I sounded a bit abrupt."

"That's all right. Always glad to help the police. But about that Mr. Gower. I hope he's in no real trouble."

"Heavens, no! He just doesn't want to be a witness against a friend. Which reminds me. We think he's here in town, so if he should get into touch with you, just give us a confidential ring."

Maylock said he certainly would. And then he had to cast yet another last, lingering look behind. "He was a nice young gentleman. A lot of class about him."

"I know," Jewle told him soberly. "His father, as you said, is a very well-known man."

Maylock showed us through the main entrance. We took the stairs, not the lift.

I had a whole lot of questions to ask but I didn't want to sound too eager. "Maylock has a pretty good investment here?"

"Just a nice little business. Nothing like the big boys. Probably confined largely to the Market trade. A pretty clean nose as far as I remember."

We were in Churston Street again. Jewle looked about him for a moment. "Now I'm here I think I'll slip along to Division. Rather use their phone than Maylock's."

He glanced at his watch. "Look. That's Havelock Street There's a pub, the Crown and Anchor, just round the corner where they do a pretty good lunch. You fix up a table and I'll join you there."

The pub was uncomfortably full. There wouldn't be a table for at least ten minutes, so I ordered a tankard and stood there by the bar. A lot of things were puzzling me but not why Jewle had gone to Divisional Headquarters. He'd be phoning from there to get enquiries started at Gower's old address—the Excelsior Hotel. There was the chance, of course, that he might want more information about Maylock, and where better to get it than in his own bailiwick.

I'd just managed to get a table when Jewle came in. While we were waiting for the soup to arrive he gave me quite a quizzical look.

"You're looking like a dog who's forgotten where he's buried the bone. Something worrying you?"

I had to smile.

"Didn't think I was so obvious. I did happen to be thinking of how you handled Maylock."

"In what way?"

"Well, not telling him he'd had a lucky escape. Not warning him his man had been a fake."

"Oh, that," he said. "No point is giving too much information away."

I still didn't see it so I shifted ground.

"About Maylock himself. Why'd he keep harping on Gower long after you'd virtually finished? Why was he so interested?"

"Maybe natural curiosity. He's a real East-ender, you know. His old man was a pawnbroker in Bow, and he and his brother started off as bookmakers' runners. When the old man died they sold the business and started book-making in a small way. That's how Bert's got where he is now. Nothing very big but still doing nicely."

Only when he'd finished that brief biography did I realise he'd somehow been side-tracking me. I smiled.

"Good for him. All the same I doubt if that's why you didn't want to hurt his feelings by letting him know he'd as good as been taken for a ride."

The waiter arrived with the main course and took the soup plates at the same time. You got quick service at the Crown and Anchor at rush hour.

"Let's work all this out slowly," Jewle told me as he settled down. "Start with our friend Gower and you stop me if you think I'm wrong. Gower came to London after that Bournemouth job. He had money in his pocket and jewellery he hoped to dispose of. Things looked so good he decided to have a flutter. Not with the really big boys. Rumour has it some of them don't like welshers. All right then. So he unearthed Maylock's."

I was going to interrupt but he stopped me.

"I know. Maybe he wasn't thinking only of a flutter. He could have worked out some kind of swindle, like that fifty each-way bet which nearly came off. When it didn't, he left the hotel. And by my calculations he'd very little money left: just enough to pay for a week at the Chaucer where he hoped to pull off another job. He didn't have to, as we know, so he came to town again and this time with plenty in his pockets.

"Now he didn't know if Maylock would be looking for him. Even one more looking for him might be too much, so he decided to square things with Maylock. He pitched a yarn about paying him back even if it was with his last cent. And that's where it gets really interesting."

He took another bite or two before going on.

"Remember how, when the name of Maylock first cropped up, I told you it seemed to ring a bell? That's why I was so careful this morning when we saw him. Then I just learned that I'd been right. This is what happened, I think, when Gower settled with Maylock with what was said to be virtually his last cent. The last thing Gower wanted was for Maylock to know he had money. You agree?"

I did.

"Right then. Now think back again. Maylock said he'd looked Gower up. Gower was a most convincing person, so, one way and another, Maylock had swallowed all that hokum he'd been dished out. Poor Mr. Gower! A really nice young gentleman. And down almost to his last cent You know what I think Maylock told him? Something like this.

"'A gentleman like you oughtn't to find it hard to raise money. You're the only son, so you'll have plenty one of these days. I know a firm that'll oblige you. They're not robbers. A really reliable firm. And their interest rates are the lowest in the business. In case you should think about it, here's their address—The Havelock Loan and Finance Company, 73 Havelock Road. Only a couple of hundred yards from here.'"

"I get it," I said. "Maylock was a kind of agent who'd collect a commission."

Jewle almost laughed. "Better than that. Now his brother's dead, Bert Maylock is sole owner of the so-called company. He and his brother founded the business: a money-lending business pure and simple, for all that high-flown name. Perfectly respectably conducted, I'll admit that, but purely a money-lending business all the same. And a nice lucrative circle. Maylock, the bookmaker, recommending the money-lenders to any likely client, so that that client can go on having funds to bet with."

I couldn't help smiling. "A nice little set-up. But wait a minute. You think Gower did go to the money-lenders?"

Jewle hoped he did.

"Let me clear something else up first, in case it hasn't occurred to you. The beauty of that combination of bookmaker and money-lender is this. When there's a welsher, a bookmaker has no legal means of recovery. A money-lender has. Maylock therefore had a kind of insurance. But about Gower. He might have had quite a lot of money at the time but my judgment is that he also had quite a sense of irony. Put yourself in his shoes. Maylock has accepted you. He's swallowed all you've told him and now he's virtually offering you more money. Wouldn't you be a fool not to take it?"

He was dead right.

"So what do we do now?"

"Lie low for a few hours," he said. "Later this afternoon I'll ring Maylock. I'll tell him very guardedly I have a suspicion that that Gower business looks as if it's been amicably settled. I may learn something from how he takes it, and I may not. If Gower did arrange a loan, then Maylock won't have anything to worry about. I don't think he was worrying this morning. I think I handled him sufficiently well."

Maybe I was being a bit obtuse but I still didn't get the full hang of it all. Jewle did some more explaining.

"Maylock's manager at the loan company is a cousin, a man named Hackle. Joe Hackle. If I'd let Maylock know Gower was a fake, he'd by now have rung Hackle and told him to get busy finding Gower. I don't want him to ring Hackle, and for the simple reason that the whole thing's going to be sprung on him when we pay an unexpected visit to that loan company."

The bread and cheese had disappeared and the waiter was hovering ominously near. People, probably from the Market, were still waiting for tables, so Jewle paid the bill and we left.

"Let's run an eye over that loan company's premises," he said.

We strolled the few yards with an eye for 73. His information was that it was above a florist's shop and it wasn't hard to find. We crossed the street and had a look at the names on the board in the side passage. The loan company shared the first floor with what could only be a private detective agency—Hewes Investigations, Ltd.

"You heard of them?" Jewle said.

I said I seemed vaguely to remember seeing the name among the advertisements in one of the popular Sunday papers.

"You don't think there's any connection?"

"If there isn't, then it's a chance lost," he said. "Loan companies get bilked often enough."

We walked back to the end of Havelock Street, the temporary parting of the ways.

"I'll give you a ring later," he said. "Mayn't be till about half-past five."

He rang me bang on the dot.

"I've just given the glad news to Maylock," he told me. "I'm pretty sure he's never mistrusted Gower for a single second. That means he never saw fit to talk to Hackle after our call this morning. So this is what I'd like you to do. For all I know Hackle might spot me but he won't know you. If we've had bad luck and Maylock *has* told him about this morning's visit, then you'll have to play it accordingly. If you're pretty sure the news you're going to give him is going to be a shock, then play it straight. You're who you are and you're looking for Gower. That suit you?"

I said it suited me fine.

4
THE ALLY

THERE comes a time in a good many cases when you get the feeling that things are going none too well. Overnight I'd regarded that call on the Havelock Loan and Finance Company as something really promising in the hunt for Gower, but in the morning I woke with no real heart for it. I didn't see where it could lead us. Even at the best, all it could produce was the knowledge that Gower had added that loan company to his list of swindles, and if we were simply to follow the same methods with the hope that some ultimate swindle would be the one too many, then the case would go dragging on for weeks or months.

Still, I made my way to Havelock Street and it was just about half-past ten when I mounted the side stairs of Number 73. The loan company occupied almost the whole of that fairly large first floor. Hewes Investigations Ltd. were across to the right. I rapped on the door marked Enquiries and went in. An elderly secretary was tackling a cup of tea and she put it hastily down. I asked if I could see the manager.

"You have an appointment?"

"No," I said, and gave her an agency card. "But I think he'll see me. It's rather important."

The agency card had shaken her a bit.

"Do you mind waiting a minute, sir? I'll speak to the manager myself."

I reminded her to tell Mr. Hackle the call was important. She gave me a quick look when I mentioned the name. She went through a door to the right and I had a quick look round. There was nothing shoddy about that enquiry office. It was quite spacious and nicely furnished. It was probably used partly as a waiting-room.

The secretary was opening the door and asking me to go through. Hackle's desk was by the far wall. That gave him a chance for a quick, preliminary appraisal of a client as he made the good fifteen feet across. The room itself was coldly efficient: a vinyl-covered floor with a reproduction Bokhara in front of the desk: a row of filing cabinets, a massive safe and four chairs. There were wall shelves with reference books, a clock and a calendar but no pictures. And no flowers.

Hackle himself looked the essence of efficiency. Money-lending might be thought to have its seamy side, but there was nothing seamy about Joseph Hackle. He was dressed in the best city tradition: dark jacket, dark tie in a lighter waistcoat, and striped trousers. He looked in the late fifties: hair slightly greying and the least bit of a stoop in the shoulders. He was clean-shaven, and his complexion on the reddish side as if he shaved too closely. The eyes were cold in spite of his smile.

"Mr. Travers?" He leaned across the desk with an out-stretched hand. "I'm Hackle, the manager here. Just what can I do for you, sir?"

I helped myself to a chair.

"To be perfectly frank, I think I have some bad news for you. This conversation, by the way, is in strict confidence, so you can talk as freely as I can."

He moistened his lips. He must have heard quite a few bombshells in his time, and you could almost see him wondering just what kind of explosion was about to occur. "You said bad news?"

"Yes, about a man whom I have reason to believe you accepted as a client. Tell me quite frankly; haven't you had dealings recently with an Edward Gower?"

The answer was pat, and expected. His smile was practically a commiseration. "You know, sir, I can't answer you that. I don't say for a moment that the man you've mentioned was one of our clients but where'd we be if—"

"Just a moment. Let me spare you some time. You're about to tell me precisely what Mr. Maylock told Superintendent Jewle of Scotland Yard and myself yesterday morning, that it isn't ethical to divulge a client's name. Well, he did divulge the name. So why not answer my own question?" He thought pretty hard. My knowledge of Maylock had been a shock.

"Well, even assuming he was a client, how does that concern yourself?"

I told him. He was incredulous, then he was agitated, but by the time I'd finished there'd come over him a considerable relief. I guessed why.

"I think you acted under Mr. Maylock's direct instructions," I told him. "I'd say that the self-styled Gower came here late on the Wednesday morning and that you had everything ready for him to sign. How much did you lend him?"

He moistened his lips again. "Five hundred pounds."

"I don't want the details," I said. "What you've told me is what I wanted to know. Mind if I use your phone?"

I rang the Yard and in a few moments was talking to Jewle. I took care to address him by name. When he'd rung off I still made as if I was listening. I came out with a *yes* or two and an *of course* before I rang off.

"Tell me," I asked Hackle, "what do you do when you're the victim of a swindle like this?"

"It's the first time such a thing has occurred. I shall have to think. Probably we shall start enquiries. If we catch up with him he'll either have to repay together with all expenses or be taken to court"

"Who usually conducts your enquiries? Your neighbour—Hewes?"

"Yes." he said. "We do employ Mr. Hewes. We have done for many years. Why'd you ask?"

"Because I'm as anxious as you are to lay hands on Gower. I can furnish him with additional person descriptions and various other things which he couldn't get elsewhere."

He got up from his chair. "That's very good of you. He's just across from the lobby. I'll show you."

My guess was that at the moment he didn't care a couple of straws if I saw Hewes or not. What he did want was to get me out of that office and be left free to talk to Maylock. Another guess was that there'd be quite a lot of talking to do. At any rate I went across the small lobby to Hewes Investigations Ltd. What I didn't know was that I was about to have one of the most interesting encounters of a pretty long career.

I gave the bell a push. I didn't actually hear it ring but I thought I heard from inside a voice inviting me to enter, so I opened the door and stepped in. I went through a small waiting-room. The door of the room ahead was ajar. Along the wall to the right was a desk, and behind it was a big man in a swivel chair. He glanced up, and no more. The sound he was making couldn't be called lugubrious: it was a cross between humming and groaning—I mean that's what it sounded like to me. Call it a personal accompaniment to his thoughts.

On the desk had been quite an array of travel folders which he was now gathering up and literally scooping into a drawer. I could identify only one, which was of the French Riviera, and I recognised it because a travel agency with whom we have dealings had sent me one like it. He closed the drawer and looked up. The whole business hadn't taken more than a few seconds.

I'd like you to run, as I did, a quick eye over Norman Hewes. He looked well into the sixties; a tall, immensely powerful man, heavy-jowled and with thin, greying, sandy hair. His long fingers were slightly spatulate and there was sandy hair on the backs of his hands, and his shoulders had the least bit of a stoop. His face was the sallowish-grey of a city-dweller. He looked like a man who'd take his time over things: not necessarily a ponderous man but a careful one. His clothes were just a bit loose on him. and their unbrushed appearance gave a faint air of seediness or disillusionment. It came as quite a surprise that he should be smiling as he got briskly to his feet.

"Mr. Travers, isn't it?" He held out a huge hand. "Glad to make your acquaintance, sir."

The cool hand enveloped my own like a muff. There was a slight turgidity in his voice. Bronchial trouble, maybe.

"You know me?"

"By sight, sir, yes. The last time I saw you, you were giving evidence at the Old Bailey. In the Marget case. Take a seat, sir. Make yourself comfortable."

The room was about twelve by nine and, except that everything had a slightly worn look, it was a replica of a dozen such offices into which I'd stepped in my time. I reached for a chair and drew it up."

"That was quite a time ago," I said. "You're Mr. Hewes, I take it."

"That's right, sir—Norman Hewes." He waved a slow hand round. "A bit of a come-down, so to speak, from that place of yours in Broad Street."

"Now, now," I said. "You mustn't say things like that. We're all in the same line of business. In any case I'm glad to meet you."

He smiled to himself. "I always like remembering faces. Faces are things I never forget. It's a gift, I reckon. Some have it and some don't."

He seemed to pull himself together as if he knew he was talking to himself. For his size it was quite briskly that he got to his feet.

"You'd like a cup of coffee, sir. I always have one myself about now."

I said that was very good of him. There was a cupboard just across in the corner with a small electric heater. By it was another door. From what I could see it was a kind of cloak-room with wash-basin. He filled the kettle there. He brought a couple of cups to the desk, with sugar and an unopened bottle of milk, and all the time he'd been talking in his unhurried way. He'd been on the Southampton force, he said, but had had to retire through ill-health. Then this opening had presented itself and he'd taken it. That was fifteen years ago. Hackle, it appeared, was a distant relation.

"You work pretty closely with the loan company, I take it?"

He said he did. There was also a reasonable amount of other work. He had one regular man—now out on a job—and a couple of other men he could call on if need be.

The kettle was boiling. The coffee, of course, was too hot to drink, so after a sip I set my cup down.

"Nice to hear you're doing so well," I told him. "The loan company gets quite a few welshers?"

"Well, yes. They all do."

"But you catch up with most of them?" I smiled. "I'm not being inquisitive. Just interested. It just doesn't happen to be one of our particular lines."

"It's generally pretty easy," he said. "You see there are certain known facts from the start. I'd say our record is well over ninety per cent."

He drank some of the coffee. Mine was still pretty hot. And if you're wondering why we were having all this preliminary chatter, I can only say—impersonally, if I may put it that way—that my call was for him something of an event. We were just two men in the same line of business comparing notes: I in no particular hurry, and he with all the time in the world. And glad of a break in monotony.

He finished his coffee and set down the cup with an appreciative breath. "And now, sir, I take it you came to see me about something."

I told him—confidentially for the moment—all the facts: Gower's record, the Newmarket swindle, the call on Maylock and my talk with Hackle. He sat still as a computer, just taking everything in.

"A smart operator," he said. "Funny, though, that the police haven't caught up with him after all this time."

He took down Gower's description. He was inclined to agree with my idea that he was an amateur.

"You think the loan company will want you to get to work at once?"

"No doubt of it," he said.

"And in view of what I've told you, you think you'll be starting off with a chance?"

"Why not?" he said. "You'll pardon me, but we've ways and means that a set-up like your own never hears about. I think we've more than an even chance."

I did some quick thinking. "Look, Mr. Hewes, I'd like to have an understanding with you. In view of that Newmarket business and to satisfy my client, I'd naturally like to be in on it early if you do happen to run down Gower. I'm not suggesting anything unprofessional, but you see what I mean."

He pursed his thick lips. "Yes, sir," he said slowly. "I think that could be managed."

"Naturally, I'd expect to pay for it," I told him. "Just between ourselves. You let me know where Gower can be got into touch with and I'll pay you—what shall we say?—twenty-five pounds?"

"That's generous of you. Mind you, sir, it's not going to be all that easy—finding him, I mean. He's a man with quite a lot of money in his pocket."

"True," I said. "And a man like him is going to spend it. That ought to be a clue in itself. I'm not telling you your business but I'm pretty sure he's a man who likes to bet. He may be investing some of it in betting shops."

"Yes," he said, and frowned. "I wonder why Mr. Hackle hasn't wanted me? Still, I'll see you out, sir. You don't want to see him again yourself?"

I said I didn't. At the enquiry room he gave a look in. "Mr. Hackle in?"

"No," he was told. "He went out quite a long time ago."

"Right," he said, and closed the door. He went with me down the stairs, maybe for a breath of less stuffy air.

"Where're you living, Mr. Hewes?"

"Stratford," he said. "It's handy enough. A bus goes right by this door. You live in town yourself?"

I did, I said. A flat at St. Martin's. I'd have liked to be more in the country but my wife liked it there.

"What does your wife think of Stratford?"

"I'm a widower," he said, and held out his hand. "It's been a real pleasure meeting you, sir. I hope I'll be able to get into touch."

He made his careful way back to the passage. I moved on to a bus stop. A quarter of an hour later I was back in the office and ringing Jewle.

Our operations that morning had been synchronised. He'd allowed time for me to speak to Hackle and then he'd rung Maylock, full of apologies, of course, but breaking the dramatic news. Maylock, he said, had collapsed like a burst tyre.

"You were dead right about everything," I told him. "Hackle, the loan company manager, must have been instructed to advance up to five hundred pounds. Gower was given that amount in cash and disappeared straight away. I did manage to have a word with Hewes's, the private detective, and he expects to be put on the job by Hackle."

Jewle chuckled. "Good luck to him. He stands about an icicle's chance in hell."

Naturally the police would be following everything up. Every hotelier who was a member of the association had long since been warned.

He asked if I'd got a description from Hackle. It was something I'd completely forgotten.

"Doesn't matter," he said. "Matthews has just seen both Maylock and Hackle. Gower had blond hair again this time and no moustache."

That was about everything. I'd taken care to make no special mention of Hewes. After all, he was my one hope of giving to Isabel Herne some concrete proof that her hundred and fifty hadn't been dropped down the drain. And then, over lunch, I began to have some qualms, and when I got back to the office, I talked it over in the general manager's office with Norris.

He thought we'd be doing the right thing. The police now had the matter in hand and there was nothing we could independently do. He didn't seem too happy about that arrangement with Hewes—as an ex-Yard inspector I couldn't expect him to be—but we worked out a compromise. A minute or two later I was dictating a letter to Isabel. Enclosed would be our cheque for the balance of the fee, less twenty-five pounds for future emergencies. When Bertha brought in the letter I added a postscript in my own handwriting. I told her, as an old family friend, to erase the whole affair from her mind. There was a certain amount more—largely platitudinarian—and after that letter had been posted I wished I could have had it back. It had been something that had had to be said but hardly in the way I'd said it. I wondered if she would read into it something I was now wincing at seeing myself—a certain pious smugness and a faint condescension.

I was wishing, in fact, that I'd never handled that case at all and, frankly, I was glad that, as far as we were concerned, it was now all over. As for that twenty-five pounds arrangement with Hewes, I'd have bet anyone a hundred to one in half-crowns that we never would have to pay it out.

By the next morning things were almost back to normal and the Gower affair hardly ever came to my mind. The morning after that I admit to looking carefully through my newspapers before I left for the office, but there was never a mention of Gower. At the office there was a letter from Isabel Herne, addressed to me personally. Nothing of what I'd feared had apparently been read into my own letter. She was most grateful. She was glad she'd come to Broad Street and unburdened her mind, and now she was beginning to regard the whole thing as little more than an unpleasant episode.

In some ways that was how I wanted to regard it too. At any rate for the next couple of days I thought less and less about it. Jewle did ring once to say there was still nothing to report and he was rapidly becoming of the opinion that Gower had slipped abroad. One trouble there, of course, was that it wasn't possible to check if he had a passport. All he could say definitely was that none had been issued under any of the three names by which he'd been known.

And so to the morning when I had a call. It was just after nine o'clock and I'd only had time to run a preparatory eye over the morning's mail when Bertha buzzed through to say a man was on the line. He wouldn't give his name.

She put him through and I picked up the receiver.

"The Broad Street Detective Agency," I said.

"That you, Mr. Travers? This is You-know-who."

I did know who. No mistaking the slow, slightly asthmatic voice of my friend Norman Hewes.

5
SO NEAR

"I THINK we've located a certain person. I'd say it's ten to one on. Could you meet me outside Harrods?"

"When?"

"As soon as you can," he said. "I'm ringing from there now. He's in a hotel."

I virtually sprinted for the Underground. It took just twenty minutes to get to Knightsbridge. Hewes was waiting. He looked mightily pleased with himself as he held out his hand.

"Well, sir, looks as if we've pulled it off. It's this way."

He was heading past Harrods. There was quite a lot of foot traffic. You can't talk while you're dodging your fellow pedestrians and almost at once he was taking the passageway through to Morley Street. For a man of his build he was a quick walker, but he slowed down as we went through to Mortimer Square. Then he pulled up short. He pointed.

"That's where he is—the Harringdon Hotel. Quite a posh place. That's my man there. Name of Peplow. Better talk things over here, sir. You want him and so do I, but I want him first. Once he hands over what he owes us, he's all yours. That all right with you?"

I said it was. We moved across the square to the photographer's shop where Peplow was standing by the shop window reading a newspaper. Real detective stuff. Hewes introduced me. Peplow looked nearer sixty than fifty, and had ex-copper written all over him. He said nothing had so far happened. He'd looked in the dining-room a few minutes ago and our man still wasn't down for breakfast.

"Might be having it in his room." Hewes said. "Tell you what we'll do, sir. You stay here, George. Mr. Travers and I'll have a look. If he still isn't down, we'll go up to his room. Seventy-eight, isn't it, George?"

We went through the swing doors. In the large foyer were no more than half-a-dozen people. The lift door opened and a porter was bringing out some luggage. The one clerk at the desk was explaining something to a guest. Hewes nodded back at me and we took the lift. It was automatic and we got off at the first floor. In the passage we looked at the room number-board and turned left. We stopped just short of seventy-eight.

"You stay here, sir," Hewes said. "I'll let you know when to come in. Better keep out of sight till I'm inside."

I heard him rap at the door. He rapped louder. A second or two and he rapped again. I joined him. He waved a hand for silence as he put his ear against the door.

A chambermaid came round the corner just as Hewes drew back.

"We were expecting to see a friend here," I told her, "but we can't make anyone hear."

She looked at the number. She looked at a kind of note-book she had in her overall pocket.

"This room's vacant," she told us. "It's on my list"

"It can't be!" Hewes said. "You've got a key? So that we can look in?"

"I don't know," she said. "Might be all right, though, so long as you don't go in."

She opened the door. The room might never have been occupied except for the rumpled towels hanging by the basin. The bed hadn't been slept in.

"Oh, my God!" That was Hewes. "Come along, sir. Let's get down and see what we can find out there."

The lift was free.

"Can't make it out," he said. "There couldn't have been a slip-up. We had everything taped."

"Look," he said, when we stepped out to the foyer. "You do the talking, sir, and I'll listen."

There was no one at the desk. I asked the clerk if we could see the manager. He ran a quick eye over us before picking up the house phone. He still didn't press the button.

"Is it important, sir? Nothing I can't see to myself?"

I told him firmly we had to see the manager. I'd prefer it if he joined us at the desk. We had to wait a couple of minutes before he arrived. I'd moved a few feet back. He gave me a highly suspicious look after he'd inspected the agency card.

"What is this? Just why are you here?"

"This is a colleague, Mr. Hewes," I said. "We're pretty sure you've been entertaining a highly dangerous guest. We've just been up to his room but he seems to have gone. He was the occupant of seventy-eight."

"Dangerous? What d'you mean by dangerous?"

"We think he was a crook," I told him patiently. "He has a record of hotel swindles and thefts."

He went back to the desk at once. He examined the register. He had a word with the desk clerk and then used the house phone. A youngish woman appeared— she turned out to be a desk receptionist—and he went to meet her. They came back to the desk and the register was again inspected. It was a good couple of minutes before he joined us where we were waiting in the background.

"Seventy-eight checked in six days ago," he said. "He registered in the name of Brian Norton of Sydney,

Australia. British. He checked out last night at about nine-thirty."

Behind me Hewes gave a little grunt.

"Mind checking if he had a telephone call during the evening."

He used the house phone to check.

"This is bloody awful," Hewes told me. "It just can't have happened. I tell you we had him dead to rights."

"No panic," I told him. "If he's gone, he's gone. We've got to try and find out where."

Gower had had a telephone call that previous night and he'd taken it in his room at about a quarter-past nine. A few minutes later he'd checked out.

"How'd he pay his bill? By cash or cheque?"

He conferred with the receptionist. The bill had been paid in five-pound notes.

"Wait a moment," he said, "five-pound notes. You don't think there's any connection with the Big Train Robbery?"

"I doubt it," I said. "But do you mind finding out if he made any telephone calls himself? And may I use your phone?"

"Better use my office," he told me. "If he had any calls it'll be on his account."

I motioned to Hewes to stay where he was. I didn't want him to know I was going to ring Jewle.

Jewle wasn't available but I got Matthews.

"Who?" he said.

I oughtn't to have been surprised that he'd forgotten the name. As far as the Yard was concerned, Gower was pretty small fry.

"Oh, him," he said. "Something happened?"

I explained. He said he'd be along straight away.

The manager was still making enquiries. A moment or two and he was telling me that our man had made no calls. Four had been received.

"And now what's all this about?"

There was something else I wanted him to do: see that seventy-eight was left untouched. A man from the Yard would be along soon and there ought to be some fingerprints. All very discreet, I told him. There'd be no scandal. Nobody would even know we'd been there.

He was a pretty perturbed man when I told him all about Gower. I said he ought to be a happy one. Gower, we knew, had been in funds or he might have left without paying his bill and maybe with the contents of a ransacked room or two.

"Anywhere quiet my man and I can talk?"

"The dining-room'll be free. You'd like some coffee?"

I didn't have to ask Hewes to bring Peplow in. He'd thought ahead of me and the two were waiting by the desk. I made a suggestion Peplow should find the hall porter who'd handled Gower's luggage and try and trace the taxi that had taken him away. Hewes and I adjourned to the dining-room. The manager had already arranged for coffee. It arrived almost at once.

"Right," I said to Hewes. "Tell me all about it. Start at the very first whisper and take your time."

He admitted he'd thought that betting shop idea of mine a likely one, so he'd got busy that very afternoon after Hackle had told him to find Gower. He'd done quite a lot of investigations at betting shops and knew quite a few managers, but it wasn't till the previous early afternoon that he'd struck oil. A man of Gower's description had used a betting shop in Quincy Street the previous day and he'd already placed a bet there that afternoon.

"Just a minute," I said. "You said he answered to Gower's description. But what about his accent?"

"He didn't say anything about an Australian accent. He said a posh accent, like you'd expect from Gower. After all, sir, he wouldn't have anyone to convince at a betting shop. He'd keep that for the hotel."

Hewes had sent Peplow along. Gower was still there and he answered closely enough to Hackle's description for Peplow to check quickly inside and then keep a watch. He also rang Hewes from a restaurant across the street. Racing ended with the four-thirty and Gower emerged soon afterwards. It was only a five-minute walk to the hotel. Peplow was close behind him when he collected his key at the desk, but he didn't follow him up to his room. Gower's movements from then on were easy to follow. Just after six o'clock he came down, bought a late special at the foyer stand, read for a time and then adjourned to the bar. He got into conversation there with a couple of guests and it wasn't till just after eight that he went to the dining-room. Peplow rang Hewes and reported.

"And that's where I went wrong," Hewes said. "Believe me, Mr. Travers, I could—I could break my own damn neck for it. You see George rang me again just before nine and said Gower'd gone upstairs again. I reckoned it had to be for the night. It looked as if we had him nicely bottled up so I told him to go home and be back at eight the next morning—this morning. I got here about a quarter to nine and then I rang you."

I saw Matthews coming through the swing doors and went to meet him. He had a young sergeant with him: a quiet-looking young fellow named Olton. I had to give another quick review and then we joined Hewes. Matthews wanted his version so I had to listen to the whole thing again. Hewes's explanation and apologies weren't going down particularly well, but it wasn't till Hewes had finished that Matthews erupted.

"You and your loan company! Know what you were doing? Cutting corners to get your personal pound of flesh instead of getting in touch with us. You knew we wanted him. And don't say you didn't."

Hewes stood up for himself. All he'd done was carry out orders. I had to smile to myself when he told Matthews, with a considerable dignity, that he—Hewes—was an employee and not a principal.

"I know. Theirs not to reason why. But don't kid yourself. You're not in the clear. Nor is Hackle. By the way, where's that man of yours—Peplow?"

I explained. Matthews left Olton to take over and we saw the manager again. His name, by the way, was Grenson. He was tall and quite distinguished-looking. He'd been over thirty years in the hotel business and had graduated from the Savoy. Matthews tried to look suitably impressed.

The three of us went upstairs. The room was just as I'd last seen it. With Grenson's permission Matthews took possession of the drinking glass on the basin shelf. The newspaper Hewes had mentioned was in the waste-paper basket and he took that, too. We had a look in the chest of drawers and the wardrobe. Nothing was there, but something peculiar was striking me about the bed. I asked Grenson if he'd find out what time the previous night the chambermaid had given it a final touch-up. He used the room telephone.

"Half-past seven," he told us. "It's a rule here that all bedrooms have to be finished while guests are at dinner."

"You ran across this Brian Norton yourself?" Matthews asked him.

Grenson had no knowledge at all. The Harringdon was a large hotel with a constantly changing clientele. It would be only when an emergency cropped up or some personal problem of a guest, that he'd have any direct contact.

"Who would have had contact with him?"

Grenson said the best person to question would be his personal waiter.

"Then he's the one we'd like to see. Think you could have him in your office for us? We'll be down in a couple of minutes."

The door closed on Grenson. Matthews wanted to know why I'd seemed interested in the bed.

"He had at least one bag," I said, "so where did he pack it? I don't know what you do but I always put mine on the bed. This bed hasn't even a ruck in it, so, after what Grenson told us, Gower probably had it packed before half-past seven. If so it can only mean that even before he received that telephone call, he knew he was practically certain to be leaving here."

"Yes," he said. "I'd something else in mind that seems to have the same bearing. A chap like Gower wouldn't have come up to his bedroom at nine o'clock. He'd have been far more likely to go out on the town or put in an hour or two in the bar. As you say, he was expecting that call."

"And since he was going, all the call would tell him was where exactly to go."

"Right," Matthews said. "Let's get downstairs and hear what that waiter's got to tell us."

In the lift I thought of something else. Everything we'd so far learned of Gower was that throughout his short but profitable career he'd consistently been a lone wolf.

Now apparently he had an ally—the overnight caller. There was no time to argue the point. In the foyer Olton and Hewes were still awaiting the return of Peplow. We went on to Grenson's office.

A word in your ear. Pretty dull work, you may think— for you, that is. But not for us. What seems routine is pretty exciting to us. Even a triviality might turn out to be of consequence. We weren't to know it then, but practically everything that had happened in the last twelve hours, even if only vaguely connected and surmised rather than understood, was later on to be of vital importance. Even the waiter had something to contribute.

He was an experienced man: a Swiss who was introduced as Frederick. His English was remarkably good.

Whenever he was on duty he had had Norton's table on his list. He had liked him—as guests go. He had been friendly—asked what his Christian name was, for instance—and had obviously been a gentleman: far more so than some Australians with whom he'd had to deal.

"You accepted him as an Australian?"

"Why, yes, sir." He smiled. "Here we get what you call all sorts. One recognises the accents."

"Just describe him to us. As you saw him."

Frederick looked up at the ceiling and thought Mr. Norton, he said, was about five feet ten and good-looking. His hair was a light-brown—almost a Scandinavian blond. He couldn't be sure but he thought the eyes were light-brown too. His face was very tanned.

"Did he talk to you about himself?"

Frederick did some more thinking. There'd been no real conversation till the previous day—at lunch. Mr. Norton had asked him if he knew Italy. Frederick had never been there. He asked if Mr. Norton was going there and he said he was. Maybe in the course of the next day or two. He had some relatives there.

That was all we learned. In the foyer the errant Peplow had at last returned. Matthews told Olton to take the glass and paper to the Yard and then come back. The results from the prints should be phoned to the hotel. The rest of us, except Grenson, retired to a corner. Peplow was looking rather pleased with himself. Hewes, still standing, maybe, on his dignity, was a bit glum. A few minutes and we were to learn precisely why.

Peplow had done a highly efficient job. He'd first seen the hall-porter who'd handled Norton's luggage—two fairish-sized bags easily carried by hand. The cab rank at Howard Street—not more than a quarter of a mile away—had been rung and a taxi arranged while the guest was paying his bill. The cab rank was constantly being rung from the hotel when a guest wasn't in too much of a hurry. The driver who turned up was known as Stan—a middle-aged man with a straggly moustache.

Peplow hot-footed it to the cab rank. Stan was out, so he waited. It was almost half an hour before he turned up. He remembered picking up an Australian gentleman just before half-past nine the previous night and he'd been told to go to Victoria station. It had been an easy trip: only about twenty minutes. Just as they were nearing Victoria the fare had asked to be set down at the Continental end. Stan had helped with the bags which had been taken over by a porter. He hadn't thought he'd be able to identify the porter.

Matthews did some thinking. Did I want Peplow or Hewes again? I said I didn't.

"Right," Matthews said. "We're much obliged to you, Mr. Peplow. You may have saved us quite a lot of time. You too, Mr. Hewes. If we should need statements, we know where to get you."

We watched them go through the swing doors. I'd just got out the first word of a remark when Matthews cut me off.

"The Continental platforms. They're to the left as you come in. Might save time if we rang."

The foyer was uncommonly busy, what with arrivals and departures. Grenson's office, by comparison, was peace itself. He told us to go ahead. He was going to the kitchens in any case.

Matthews rang Enquiries at Victoria. They were busy there, too. It took ten minutes to get what he wanted.

"It fits in," he said. "There's a ten-fifteen from Victoria which connects with the midnight boat for Calais. Looks as if things were getting too hot and he decided to skip."

Olton looked in. Before he'd hardly time to open his mouth, the buzzer went. Matthews picked up the receiver. A grunt or two and a final thanks and he put the receiver back.

"Our man's prints all right." he said. "Not a shadow of doubt."

He got to his feet. "Don't see what else you can do here," he told me. "We'll do a bit more grubbing around. You're going to be in your office the rest of the day? Only in case the Old Man may want to have a word with you."

I told him I'd be in—unless something told me to skip the country too. He didn't smile. In his younger days Matthews used to make joking almost a pest. He's moved the other way since then: just a bit too much on his dignity. At Broad Street nowadays we don't get very much help from Matthews. For him it's strictly the straight and narrow. Maybe he's right. I wouldn't know.

I made my way back to Knightsbridge and caught a Liverpool Street bus. It was almost empty on top, and I could have had almost any seat to myself. For once I wasn't interested in the scenery. What I wanted to do was think.

The more I thought, the more things seemed too pat. Why should the so-called Norton, hitherto not particularly loquacious, tell the waiter about a visit to Italy? Being set down near a Continental departure platform meant very little. Norton could have taken his luggage over again, on some pretext or other, from the porter and have made his way to the main entrance and there taken a taxi to anywhere. Or he could have humped the not too heavy bags to Victoria Street and taken a chance on a taxi there. In other words, he might now be anywhere. If Matthews weren't particularly dense, he'd soon be of the same opinion.

Thinking of Matthews made me remember something I wished I'd thought of at the hotel. That tanned face of Norton's. That must have come from a brisk use of a lamp, so maybe the chambermaid might have caught sight of it. Those lamps, of course, were nowadays pretty small, so maybe Norton had kept his locked up in a suitcase. All the same, it might have been worth a spot of investigation.

I'd taken a bus rather than the Underground because I'd wanted to think, and before I was dropped near Broad Street I'd done quite a lot more. By then the whole thing had crystallised into what seemed to me one question—for whose call had Norton been waiting that night in the bedroom? And, as a rider, why? Had he taken on a partner with the idea of going into business in a bigger way? If so it might turn out all to the good. A team of two should be easier to pick up than a lone operator.

When I got back from lunch I'd hardly settled down to work when there was a call. As I picked up the receiver I knew it would be either Matthews or Jewle. It was neither.

"Thought you might be in, sir." It was Hewes. "I wanted to tell you how upset I am about that fiasco this morning. Believe me, sir—"

"No need for apologies," I told him. "And, by the way, I shouldn't take Inspector Matthews too seriously. I don't think there'll be any trouble for you."

He sighed a bit heavily. "Glad to hear it, sir. That's the last thing we want. An expensive business for me already, you know, sir. I reckoned I had that twenty-five pounds of yours as good as in my pocket."

"Tough luck," I said. "Still, you may get a second chance."

"Ah!" he said. "That's what I wanted to mention to you, sir. All that business at Victoria. Do you think it might have been a blind?"

"Why, yes," I said, and let myself be surprised. "Now you mention it, I do."

"Then if he's still in town, there's still a chance."

"Looks like it," I told him. "My offer still holds good. But a word of advice. If you start making enquiries at Victoria and elsewhere, mind your step. Keep well out of Inspector Matthews's hair."

He gave a slightly asthmatical chuckle. "That's all right, sir. I can take care of myself. Thanks all the same."

I didn't want any more palaver, so I rang off. If I was smiling, it was at the eternal optimism in the breast of Norman Hewes. Even supposing that our man had doubled back, there seemed no easy way of catching up with him. A chance like that betting shop encounter wasn't likely to present itself again. And when Hewes had talked to me in his office about special ways and means, that, I thought, had been largely for the purposes of making an impression—to show that even the little fellows could have quite a few tricks up their sleeves.

The next thing that happened was not till about five o'clock when Matthews rang. Over the past two years, he said, no passport had been issued to a Brian Norton. Enquiries were still going on at Victoria but he, too, was now of the opinion that all that taxi business had been nothing but a blind.

"Naturally we can't disregard it entirely," he said. "He may be somewhere on the Continent. We're handing it over to Interpol, just in case. Don't expect anything to happen. If it does, I'll give you a ring. Won't be just yet, though."

So there it was. I'd retired gracefully from the case: paid off the client and had an interest merely academic from then on. If I'd been asked what I expected. I'd have said that at some future date—weeks ahead or even months—my Edward Gower would make the one false move. But now everything was somehow different. In a way I'd had quite an exciting morning. In a curious way I'd been in close contact with the missing Gower and I knew it would be quite some time before I could get him wholly out of my mind. In that sense, the case for me was still very much alive.

PART II

6
HENRY MORCHARD

MINE is a flibberty-gibbity, crossword-addict sort of mind, and that may account for what may seem the queer titles I sometimes give to cases in which I've taken a hand. You may be wondering, for instance, why this particular case is called The Case of the Jumbo Sandwich. Let me explain.

I happened suddenly to feel hungry one late morning when I'd been working in the suburbs and by chance I saw a snack-bar that looked new and reasonably inviting, so I went in. I asked for coffee and a chicken sandwich. The proprietor was an up-and-coming sort of man.

"You tried our Jumbo sandwich, sir?"

"I haven't. Just what is it?"

He lifted the lid of the glass container and used the slice to draw one out. It turned out to be the best sandwich I'd ever eaten. It consisted of four very large slices of bread, cut fairly thin, and buttered. Between them were three layers: the first thinly sliced sausage, then chicken and finally ham. There was seasoning, of course, and the whole thing was a happy marriage. Everything went so well together. It was delicious.

Mind you, it could have been called three sandwiches in one but if it had been three sandwiches, you'd have needed two more slices of bread. You didn't need a knife and fork for it. It wasn't so large that you couldn't bite into it and, almost as soon as you tasted the sausage, you were in the chicken, and, by the time you knew it was chicken, you were tasting the ham. Call the whole thing what you like: one large sandwich or three in one. Three separate sandwiches that overlapped.

And that's precisely what this case was going to be. It had three parts: not separate but always connected with each other. The parts overlapped. The first part had been the Edward Gower affair but, before that was finished with, along came another part. That second part began with Henry Morchard.

I've sometimes thought, not too seriously, of acquiring for myself a certain status by suggesting to the secretary that I must be among the oldest members of my club. My father put me up when I was eighteen, which was a goodish time ago, and since then I've consistently made use of it: in fact I should be presented with a problem if the club ever ceased to be.

Mind you, ancient though I'm rapidly becoming, there are far more members unknown to me than known. The old die and the young come in: you might, in fact, call it a constant turnover. Henry Morchard, for instance, was quite unknown to me. I suppose I'd seen his name among the list of members, but, if so, I'd forgotten it; in fact it conveyed nothing to me when he rang me at the office just two days after that fiasco at the Harringdon Hotel.

"The Broad Street Detective Agency," I said. "Travers speaking."

"Ah, Mr. Travers; this is Henry Morchard. I've seen you occasionally at the club but I don't think we've actually met."

"No," I said. "I don't think we have."

"Well, I'd like to give myself that pleasure. Are you free for lunch at the club?"

"Today? Yes," I said. "Shall we say half-past twelve?"

"Splendid." There was a short pause. "There's something I'd like to consult you about."

"You mean professionally?"

"Frankly, yes. I shall be most grateful. It's a highly confidential matter but there should be plenty of privacy at the club."

"Oh, yes," I said. "The library's generally free. Rather a sad comment on us, but it is."

He chuckled. "Indeed, yes. In any case I shall look forward to seeing you."

As soon as I'd replaced the receiver I began some quick thinking. Somewhere or other the name Morchard rang a vague bell. *Debrett* would be no good to me so I tried *Who's Who*. There was a Lydia Morchard there but no Henry. And I certainly knew Lydia Morchard. Bernice had dragged me along one afternoon to hear her give a talk on the American woman. The reference book told me she was president of the Home Protection League. It mentioned three important committees on which she'd served. She'd also contested a by-election, unsuccessfully, as Liberal candidate just over a year ago. And I remembered seeing her on television.

But Lydia, of course, might have no possible connection with Henry, and he was the one about whom I wanted to know a whole lot more. Then I did what I've occasionally done before—rang a Fleet Street friend. He asked if it would be all right if he rang me in about an hour.

He was rather longer than that but he had all that I wanted and more. Henry Morchard was Chairman of Morchard and Hulme, manufacturing chemists, whose plant was at Sevenoaks. It was quite a large concern with a branch in Canada. The shares were quoted in the current issue of the *Financial Times*. He was educated at Winchester and Trinity.

"You probably know his wife," he said. "Lydia Morchard."

"Of course. But I didn't know her husband was this Henry Morchard."

"Look," he said, "it's a funny thing you should have rung but I'm thinking of doing an article on her for a woman's magazine. She's standing again as Liberal candidate at the General Election whenever that is. Just how much do you want to know?"

"Between ourselves, all you've got."

"Right," he said. "I'm just about to get busy on a family tree. It makes a good framework to work from. I'll send you a copy." That was as far as I could go. Maybe I wouldn't need the information after all, but it pays to be careful. What Morchard's problem might be I had no idea, except that it was personal. And then, letting that mind of mine run on, I found myself smiling. I was wondering what it was like to be married to something of a celebrity. What would it be like to overhear yourself referred to as Lydia Morchard's husband?

I imagined that Morchard must have made some shrewd and confidential enquiries about me from some mutual friend at the club. At any rate he approached me as soon as I entered the bar. He was tall and generally as good-looking a man as I'd seen in quite a time. His hair had more grey than black, and I put his age at about sixty.

"I think I have seen you here," I told him. "Didn't know who you were, of course."

"I'm a busy man," he said. "Lucky if I can make it once a week."

He seemed to take it for granted that I, too, had made enquiries.

"Our plant is at Sevenoaks, you know."

"You live there?"

"Yes," he said. "Where my father lived before me. A place with the rather banal name of The Cedars. Not much more than a stone's-throw from the cricket ground."

We finished our sherries and went through to lunch. We took the communal table so there was no chance for private talk. Coffee we took in the library with the room virtually to ourselves. He began with a curious abruptness.

"You know my wife?"

"Naturally," I said. "She's what's known as a prominent public figure. Also my wife and I attended a lecture she gave last year."

He nodded. "You're a Cambridge man like myself. Did you know Cedric Palling?"

I smiled. "Who didn't?"

"Yes," he said. "He was very much of an eccentric. Towards the end he must have been very near to going off the rails. He was also a wealthy man, you know."

"He died pretty young."

"Yes. Killed in an air-raid on London in 1942. My wife is his widow."

There was nothing I could say. He was silent for a moment too.

"There was a son of the marriage—Lionel. He was thirteen at the time of our marriage and I think—in fact I'm sure—he violently resented it. He was always something of a problem. Rather unstable, like his father. Clever too. He'd been giving a lot of trouble but nothing like what happened after our marriage. We had to remove him from his school and then he said he wanted to study art in Paris. Against my better judgment he went there. He didn't come home for three years and, when I went over there myself, I found he'd never attended a single class. His mother had made him an allowance of a thousand a year and he'd been living on it. There were also some debts and I had to pay off a woman with whom he'd been living. He was only just nineteen at the time."

He pushed the empty cup aside. "I hate to have to say this, but he had a kind of criminal cunning. All repentance: you know what I mean. Also he could always twist his mother round his finger, so when he expressed a wish to study medicine at Edinburgh she arranged everything with some friends of hers there. Naturally I didn't interfere. And of course the same thing happened as had happened in Paris, or much the same. After that there was the episode of a stolen car which we managed to get hushed up. Other things, far worse, and finally I had to give my wife an ultimatum. It might have been reluctantly but she'd begun to see things my way.

"Under the terms of his father's will, everything had been left in trust to my wife with remainder to the two children. I didn't tell you but there's a daughter, Sylvia. She's two years older and married to a stockbroker. At any rate we shipped Lionel to Australia with five thousand pounds in his pocket. I had some friends there to whom he had a letter of introduction.

"I should have told you that under the terms of the will the trustees had uncommonly wide discretionary powers, so we were able to warn him that he had to settle down or else. Also he had to give a guarantee not to return to England before six years. Which brings me to my problem. I'm pretty sure he *has* returned."

I said nothing. Just waited for him to go on.

"I'll tell you why I think so. My wife's been acting very strangely these last few days. And there was something I overheard a couple of days ago when I came into the room when she was telephoning. I heard her say, 'You know I can't do that. Henry would never forgive me,' and then she looked round quickly and saw me, and changed the conversation in the most ludicrous way. In fact, I'm pretty sure Lionel's back in England and trying to get money out of her."

"What about Australia? Any news about him from there?"

"Not for at least a couple of years. I'd say he found out he couldn't make use of those friends of mine so he dropped them after a few weeks. Then they heard he was working in a racing stable near Melbourne. That was two years ago."

His cigar had gone out. He looked at it, stubbed it in the ash-tray and left it there.

"And what do you want me to do?" I said.

"I want my wife watched," he said, "and I want it done straight away. If she gets into touch with Lionel, I want him located. I mean to put a stop to this whole business once and for all. I don't know how but I'm damn-well going to try."

"I think we can do it," I told him.

"Just a minute," he said. "It's not going to be too easy. You'll need two men: one at Sevenoaks and one in town. She's standing as a candidate at the General Election so she has an office in town. At Welney House. That's one of those new blocks near St. Paul's."

"It might mean four men, allowing for reliefs. It's going to be pretty expensive."

"Look," he said. "You and I are men of our word. I'm not a poor man. When it's all over, send me your bill. I shan't question it. I've got too much at stake. If Lionel creates a public scandal, which he's likely to do, it'll do my wife incalculable harm. I'm trying to protect her against— well, against her own foolishness. Besottedness might be a better word. That's why I want you to get busy at once. I needn't tell you that you'll have to work with the utmost discretion."

He glanced at his watch. As he'd said, he was a busy man.

"Right," I said. "Everything seems to be clear. Two things you'll have to do. Send me straight away photographs of your wife and Lionel Palling. My men'll need them for identification."

"I'll do that." He got to his feet and held out his hand. "If you want me, you'll get me at the plant; Sevenoaks 10025."

I jotted the number down.

"And the contract?"

He stared. "I thought we'd settled all that. I've trusted you: now you trust me. Just send in your bill."

It was after three o'clock when I got back to the office. While I was talking things over with Norris, that family tree that had been promised arrived by special messenger. The family tree itself was a bit of a sprawl but simplicity itself to follow. There were also footnotes, and altogether it tidied up in my mind what Morchard had told me in the club. This is the whole thing cut down to size.

Lydia Chance, educated privately and at Goldsmith's, London, where she took a first in economic history, married a Cambridge don, Cedric Palling. There were two children of the marriage: Sylvia, now aged thirty-one, and Lionel, aged twenty-nine. Cedric Palling died in 1942.

Henry Morchard had married an Eleanor Harte. She died in 1947, leaving a son, Charles, who was now general manager of the Canadian branch of Morchard and Hulme. The widower and the widow, Henry Morchard and Lydia Palling, got married in 1949. There were no children of the marriage. Henry was now fifty-eight and Lydia fifty-two.

Dates didn't matter very much: it was the people themselves who counted, and what I read into the Morchard menage was this. Lionel couldn't have any great expectations from his step-father since the son in Canada would inherit. When his mother died, however—subject to the provisions of the trust—he might or might not come into a considerable sum. But his mother was only in the early fifties. Give her a reasonable expectation of life and Lionel would have a very long while to wait.

If he was really in England and so had broken the agreement not to return before six years, then he'd been rash indeed. Such an action could only prejudice the trustees. Why then had he done anything so foolish? Because, I thought, he'd exhausted both his stake of five thousand pounds and his Australian friends, and had come home with the intention of wheedling his mother into finding yet another grubstake. And he had to keep under cover so that she alone would be aware he'd broken the agreement.

I had another look at that abstract I'd made of the family history. I tried to go over in my mind everything that Morchard himself had told me at the club and it wasn't long before I knew there were things I'd neglected to ask. Had that interview taken place at Broad Street I'd have been much more searching.

The only thing to do was to get hold of Morchard at once and luckily he was in his office at the plant.

"One or two urgent matters," I said. "Lionel's sister Sylvia. Why shouldn't he be in touch with her, too?"

"Because I took her into my confidence this morning before I saw you. Sylvia's my girl, if you know what I mean. She knows the trouble he's caused. If he should try anything so foolish she'll get into touch with me at once."

"I see. I take it, by the way, that I'm to have a free hand, always subject to absolute discretion?"

He gave a little snort. "Of course. No point in keeping a dog and barking yourself."

"Then I'd also like a confidential word with her. May I have her address?"

He made no bones at all about giving it—Sylvia Fairfield, Flat 17, Stanwyck House, South Kensington.

"Harry, the husband, is a very good fellow," he said. "They've two children, by the way. The last thing I want is for them to become involved in any of this."

"I'll keep it strictly in mind," I said. "Now one other thing. Your opinion that Lionel's back in England was based on two things—the way your wife had been behaving and what you happened to overhear when she was telephoning. Now that expression she used about Henry would never forgive her. Surely if she were talking to Lionel she'd have said *your* father, not *Henry*?"

"Oh, no. I told you Lionel resented our marriage. He never addressed me as father. When he wanted to be objectionable, which was nearly always, he called me Henry."

I said I'd now got it straight. One other thing would he note. Those photographs he'd promised to put in the post that night.

"I have them here," he said. "My wife's in town so I was able to search her room."

I felt a sudden alarm. "You mean she's not coming home tonight?"

"Oh, no. She'll be home. We're dining with some friends at Tonbridge."

I breathed again. "About any photographs of Lionel. It's essential from our point of view that you note what a photograph doesn't necessarily show: colour of hair and eyes, for instance. The kind of thing that's noted on a passport photograph."

He said he'd see to it.

"And just one last thing. I imagine your wife goes to town most days. Could you give me a rough timing of her movements?"

"We both breakfast at about eight, then she takes a look at her mail. Then she catches the nine-thirty."

"She drives to the station?"

"No need," he said. "It's only three minutes' walk."

I took a description of her car and was just about to thank him and ring off, when he had a question of his own.

"When are you likely to see Sylvia? I'd like a word with her first. She'd probably be rather suspicious of a stranger."

"It's not far to go," I said. "Probably after dinner tonight. I'd like to know as much as I can before we get to work in the morning."

Bob Hallows, the third of a modest directorate, was back from a job. He's spent all his working life at the agency and now he's the key man. Norris deploys the staff and I help him out with paper work. When a private case turns up. I'm usually in charge, or, if he's free, Hallows lends a hand. His main job is handling the stuff that really keeps us going: work for a couple of insurance companies and two or three big industrial concerns.

It didn't take us long to arrange the morning's work. French, now the senior operative, was free and he'd take the Sevenoaks end. Once Lydia Morchard was on the London train, he'd take it too. We'd have been warned that she was on the way to the station and would be waiting at the London end. Either Hallows or I would join French in keeping Welney House under observation, and, if Lydia left her office, she'd be followed.

Since the photographs wouldn't arrive before half-past eight in the morning, I said I'd ring Morchard as soon as I judged he'd be at his office, and find out his wife's intentions with regard to town. If she was coming up, then she could be contacted at Cannon Street. For us to have familiarised ourselves with the Lionel Palling photograph was absolutely essential. It wasn't only a question of the mother leaving the office to meet the son: we had to take into account the other possibility—that the son might come to the office to see the mother.

We could have dispensed with a photograph of Lydia. Bertha had foraged round and come back with a full-page photograph in a glossy magazine. Lydia was tall and slim. She was dark and there was something Spanish about her except, maybe, for the prominent hook of the nose. When I got back to my room I couldn't help thinking of her as she'd been that afternoon when Bernice had pressurised me into attending that lecture.

She'd been a first-class speaker, and from somewhere or other she'd acquired all the tricks of the trade: the effective pause, the pointing finger, the ubiquitous smile, the timely quip and the apt aside. She had a fine voice and I remembered how Bernice had disagreed with me when I said it had sometimes been too strident. She'd certainly been both fluent and convincing, and because she'd taken care to be sure of her facts.

Facts, I said wryly to myself. Somehow you couldn't dissociate Lydia Morchard from facts. And I just couldn't imagine her as a mother. Or could I? The suitable text-books consulted, for instance, and everything organised: pregnancy, birth, and on to child psychology and even the symbolism of toys. And then it struck me somewhat sheepishly that I was being cheaply facetious about something of which I knew nothing at all. Lydia Morchard might have been the best of mothers, even if she had subsequently spoiled her son. At any rate, thinking of the mother reminded me of the daughter, so I rang Bernice about an early meal.

7
THUNDERBOLT

IF EVER I decide to hang in my office a monitory motto to keep me in line, it will consist of only three words— YOU NEVER KNOW.

Maybe we don't get the right clients or our job's confined to the wrong milieu. I don't know, but what I do know is that it isn't strewn with cracked skulls, empty bottles and bed-starved blondes. Most of the time it's just questioning and listening. What you hear may be gossip, hearsay, mere chit-chat, surmise, suspicion or absolute fact: churned up, prejudiced, distorted and occasionally vibrant with utter truth. None of it may be valuable or some of it may be significant. You never know.

As Holy Writ has it, you cannot tell which will prosper, this or that. What you have to do, if years of experience have taught you the trick, is to store everything away in your memory until, perhaps, some wholly new event or word touches off a reminder, and all at once you have a connection. You may even be lucky enough to spot the one vital and significant thing.

I wasn't expecting that night to hear anything of any great significance. I mightn't know it for such if I did. Even when I did hear it. I wasn't aware of it. Why I was calling on the Fairfields I frankly didn't know—unless it was to check up on that morning's talk between Sylvia and her father. There was also just a chance that she might have some idea of the whereabouts of her brother. If he had friends, for instance, or favourite haunts, she might know of them.

The five-storey block of flats was just behind the old Imperial Institute. Pretty long experience was telling me that the flats themselves were highly expensive ones. Morchard had given me no hint as to how the Fairfields were doing, but it wasn't unlikely, considering the warm way he'd spoken of Sylvia herself, that he was making some kind of allowance. Perhaps the mother was contributing too.

The Fairfields had obviously been expecting me. They were a delightful couple. Somehow there's become attached to the term stockbroker an idea of the boozy, the hail-fellow-well-met and the slightly moronic. Such ideas die hard. They're the ammunition of the Havenots. After all, very few of us have dealings with a real, live stockbroker.

Harry Fairfield was older than his wife: nearer forty than thirty. He talked intelligently and even amusingly.

I liked him straight away. I admit that the first thing he did after shaking hands was to offer me a drink.

Sylvia was her mother all over again: tall, dark, but just a little on the plump side. She was far better-looking than her mother had ever been: she lacked, for instance, that too aquiline nose. She smiled when I mentioned the children. They were asleep, she said and pointed across the room to a door which was just ajar.

"We have to keep our voices down?"

"Heavens no," she said. "They just sleep and sleep. We keep the door ajar just in case."

"And you like it here?"

"In some ways, yes," she said. "There's a nice little school handy for David. He's six. Susan's four. Father would like us to get somewhere out of town. Tonbridge, perhaps. He's got ideas about the country life for the children."

"Don't take this as impertinence," I said, "but I like Henry Morchard. It seemed nice, somehow, for you not to speak of him as your step-father."

"But he *is* a father! He did everything for me. He's the finest man I ever knew." She smiled. "A husband excepted."

Harry Fairfield asked if he could give me a refill. It was excellent port and I didn't refuse.

"There's a snag about Tonbridge," he said. "You married?"

"Yes. But we've no children."

"Then you wouldn't know," he said. "I mean why mothers want their daughters and sons to get married and why they often weep at the actual ceremony. They're just tears of joy: thinking about their grandchildren. Armfuls of 'em. All to be grand-mothered and smothered."

I laughed.

"You may be right," I said. "And I think I see the snag. Tonbridge is a bit too close to Sevenoaks."

"But father isn't like that," Sylvia said. "He loves the children. He's good to them but he never spoils them. You know perfectly well he never interferes."

We'd got acquainted. As in "Listen with Mother", we were all sitting comfortably and it was time to begin. My opening, I thought, was a bit subtle.

"It's a pity, Mrs. Fairfield, your brother never got round to thinking of Henry Morchard as a father."

"It was," she said. "But it was always like that with Lionel. He had to have his way. He'd go to any lengths to get his way,"

"Let's put it frankly," Fairfield said. "He was allowed to grow up with no moral conscience. Mr. Travers wants the truth and the truth is his own father put wrong ideas in his head and his mother consistently spoiled him—when she had any time for him. Believe me, Mr. Travers, you can't contract out with children. They're a full-time job."

"Yes," I said. "The whole thing's been a tragedy. And if he was spoiling only his own life it wouldn't be so bad. That's why he has to be stopped, once and for all. The essential thing, of course, is to locate him."

I put those questions about friends and haunts. They produced nothing, so I shifted ground.

"This morning I was told of some of his escapades but, strictly between ourselves, Mr. Morchard rather slurred over one thing. Just what was that final thing that made your parents decide he had to be sent out of the country?"

"It was horrible," she said. "It makes me sick when I think of it."

"I think Mr. Travers ought to know," he said. "It might give him some kind of clue. It was like this. You know Thurlow Street?"

"One of those turnings off Long Acre?"

"That's right," he said. "It comes to practically a dead end just short of Covent Garden. There's a pub called the Three Swans. The landlord was a chap called Ranmore, an ex-regimental sergeant-major. Lionel must have dropped in there and seen the daughter: a not bad-looking, flighty sort of girl who sometimes helped behind the bar. To put it crudely, he set out to seduce her. I know all this, by the way, because I helped Henry to get to the bottom of it.

"What happened was that Lionel dropped in regularly and began talking a lot about himself: how he was a newspaper-man writing a series of articles on the Garden for the American Press. He talked so big and he must have slipped up somewhere because Ranmore began to have suspicions. Also he saw what was going on between Lionel and the daughter. He was a pretty shrewd man, Ranmore, so he had enquiries made and finally he got Henry's name and actually came to see him. All I know about that was what Henry told me."

He saw a certain look on my face.

"Oh, no: that isn't the end of it. Lionel actually got the daughter to go away with him, and they were run to earth at a second-rate hotel in Ladbroke Grove. You know what Lionel did then? He used the girl as a kind of blackmail. Threatened to marry her unless he was paid off, but that time he went too far. You don't threaten a man like Henry. He just told him to go ahead. I don't know if you're aware of the conditions laid down in Cedric Palling's will, but one clause concerns the approval of any marriage by the mother, and this time Lydia had to stand firm. The upshot was that the bluff was called. Lionel was glad to settle for five thousand and leaving the country."

There was silence for a moment or two. It was, as Sylvia said, a nasty episode.

"And now he's thought to be back in England," I said. "Have you noticed anything in your mother's behaviour, Mrs. Fairfield, to give you the idea that she's aware of it?"

"It's several days since I saw her," she said. "She has so many interests. Also she's nursing a constituency, you know."

"When she does come, she sort of descends on us," Fairfield said, "just to be sure Sylvia's being the right kind of mother. You know: are you doing this: do you think you ought to do that: if I were you I'd try something else."

I smiled. "As you said, that's a grandmother for you. All part of the biological urge."

He laughed. "Biological urge be damned! If she weren't Sylvia's mother, I'd call her a damn nuisance. Luckily Sylvia takes it in at one ear and lets it go straight out through the other."

The divan was most comfortable. I had to hoist myself out of it.

"You'd like to take a peep at the children?"

I said I'd love to. I don't know why we should have had to tip-toe across a Chinese carpet, but we did. They were lovely children. No wonder the parents beamed down at them. Sylvia did some gentle tucking in and the bedroom door was left ajar again.

"If you want a testimonial for good mothership, apply to me," I said. "And thanks for seeing me. You've been very helpful."

They were charming people: the sort one wishes to see again. In the taxi that took me back to my more modest flat I tried to appraise what they had told me, and it seemed at the time that what I'd learned had been just nothing at all. But, as I've said, you never know.

I was away early in the morning. Just before half-past eight I was at Broad Street. Norris and Hallows were already there, and French was standing by for orders. The mail arrived dead on time.

I slit open the largish envelope with the Sevenoaks postmark. In it were the two photographs. That of Lydia Morchard didn't interest us. That of Lionel Palling definitely did.

It must have been taken some years back, and maybe when he was just in his twenties. It was of a young man, good-looking in an arrogant sort of way. There was a slight smile on the lips and the head was tilted a bit sideways, as if the camera was a matter of amusement. I looked at the back: "Taken at twenty-four. Height five-ten, hair light brown, eyes hazel."

I remember slowly taking off my horn-rims and beginning slowly to polish them. It was a trick I used to have when faced with a sudden decision, and I'd cured myself of it, or so I'd thought. Things began to fit in. How I could have been so obtuse as not to see them before, I didn't know.

"Take a good look at it," I said to Norris. "Who might he be?"

He didn't know. Then something dawned on him too. "You don't think it could be Gower?"

"Think of Gower's record," I said, "and compare it with Palling's. The Australian exile. The pseudo-Australian at the Harringdon. The Newmarket business. The love of a bet."

"What *is* this?" That was Hallows. He'd been away and knew nothing about a Gower.

"In a minute, Bob," I said. "There's one way of finding out if the two are one."

French was called in and given careful instructions. He was to go to Havelock Street and show the photograph to Hackle. He was to use Hackle's phone to make a report and then get back.

As I said, that likely discovery upset the whole of the morning's plans. Everything would have to be held up till after I'd seen Morchard. While it was hardly likely that he'd cease to be our client, there might be modifications on which he'd insist. Meanwhile Hallows had to be put in the picture. It wasn't hard to see the points I'd been trying to make.

"Suppose the two *are* one," he said. "What're you going to do about Jewle? Tell him about it?"

I passed the buck. Hallows shook his head. "It'll be a bit tricky. Maybe we can leave the law out of it. Keep the dual identity up our sleeves till we think suitable. After all, Jewle knows nothing about Henry Morchard and this Lionel Palling. All we're doing is working for a client. Jewle doesn't have to know all our business."

That was how we left it. It was after nine o'clock and I wanted to get into touch with Morchard, but I couldn't till we'd heard from French. And that wasn't till a quarter of an hour later.

"Sorry to be so long," he said, "but Mr. Hackle has only just got in. It's O.K. about the photograph. He's prepared to swear he's the Edward Gower he did business with."

That settled it. I had the idea that Morchard would be regularly in his office at about nine: at any rate I got him first time.

"Travers," I said. "Sorry to trouble you, but something really important has just cropped up. I've got to see you." There was a moment's silence. "It's as important as that?"

"Tremendously important. I'd like to make it as quickly as possible."

Another moment's silence. "I can't possibly get away from here. An important meeting in a few minutes' time. Could you come down here?"

"Glad to," I said. "By train. It'll be quicker than by car." He told me to hang on while he looked up trains. There was a ten-fifteen from Charing Cross and I told him I'd take it. He said there'd be a car at the station to take me on to the plant.

I'd thought I'd known Sevenoaks pretty well, but I soon discovered that I didn't know the hinterland. The Morchard and Hulme plant was a good mile away to the east on the Tonbridge side. It was much bigger than I'd imagined: ten acres perhaps, including the concrete, circular road. There was a kind of hygienic cleanliness about it all: never a chimney or a wisp of smoke. The administrative block looked very modern—three storeys of metal and glass—and in front of it was the car park of the higher-ups. My driver drew the Humber into a vacant place just in front of the entrance.

"Straight through there, sir. You can't miss it."

I went through the swing doors. Immediately on my right was a very large enquiry room. Through the glass of its front I could see the long desk that ran clean across it. A clerk was explaining something to an enquirer: another was checking some papers. To my left, as I went in, a youngish woman—clerk or receptionist—got up from her typewriter as if she'd been expecting me.

"Travers," I said, "Ludovic Travers. I think Mr. Morchard's expecting me."

She was already lifting the desk flap. "Yes, sir. Mr. Morchard will see you at once. This way, please."

She led the way along the wide passage. In the air was a faint, astringent kind of smell that reminded me of a medicine that I used to be given when I was a child. The passage turned sharp right into an immense lobby. We took a diagonal course across the rubbered floor to a door in the far corner. She opened the door and announced me.

Morchard came the few feet to meet me, hand outstretched. "More than good of you to come. Believe me. I'm most grateful. Let me take your coat. You'd like coffee?"

The wall to my left was of glass in thin metal frames and through it I could see the main entrance. But for that, the room might have been a den or library in a private house. The knee-hole writing-desk was early Georgian and the chairs matched. An eight-foot break-front book-case that looked of the same period occupied most of one wall. By a door to the right an eighteenth-century green-lacquered clock was ticking away. The wall-to-wall carpeting looked as if it had been specially woven. Half-a-dozen Morland prints decorated the walls.

"A lovely room," I said. "I wish I could do a Samson-ian act and carry it away by night."

"Well, I like it," he said. "Don't give me any credit, though. My wife was responsible for the whole thing."

"That reminds me," I said. "I meant to ask you what constituency she was standing for."

"Haversham. She did quite well there last time."

"She spends much time there?"

"At present, every Saturday. Any special reason for asking?"

"Only that it widens the area of enquiry. Her son might meet her there."

A smartly dressed, highly competent-looking woman brought in the coffee. Morchard reminded her we were on no account to be disturbed.

"This news of yours." He passed me my cup. "You said it was important."

"We judge it to be," I said. "We know for an absolute certainty, for instance, that Lionel Palling is in England, or was. He may have left a day or two ago. I don't think so. I think he's still here and almost certainly in London. I should add that he's wanted by the police."

His cup wavered in mid-air. He set it slowly down.

"The police," he said. "Doesn't that make it all the more essential we should get hold of him first? But why do they want him? What's he done?"

I started at Winchester and told him the whole story. There wasn't a single interruption. And he took it far more calmly than I'd thought.

"A dirty business. It frightens me. What's he going to become if he isn't stopped? We've got to get to him before the police. We can't afford any public scandal."

I said there were two hopeful things. We were looking for one thing and the police another. They wanted a man they knew under various aliases. What they didn't know was who he actually was. And they certainly didn't know he was in contact with his mother.

"That's true." He thought for a moment "Just in case of possibilities I think I should arrange with you to pay that woman he swindled—three thousand five hundred, you said?—and that loan company. Anonymously, of course. And provided they'll bring no actions."

I advised him not to be too precipitate. Once we caught up with his stepson, some of the money ought to be recovered.

"And your wife," I said. "Any developments?"

"It's difficult. I not only have to watch her without her knowing it, I have to watch myself. And I think she's being curiously suspicious. She asks questions about what I've been doing and where I'm going." He shook his head helplessly again. "I just don't know."

"Any physical signs of strain?"

"Yes," he said. "At breakfast this morning I thought she was looking quite ill. She said it was just a bad head-ache. Not that she—"

A queer look was suddenly on his face and he was getting to his feet. Lydia Morchard was already in the room. As I rose, she seemed to catch sight of me.

"I'm so sorry, darling. I'd no idea you weren't alone." She was so close that there was nothing to do but introduce me.

"Lydia, you know you shouldn't see me without making sure I'm free. This is Mr. Travers with whom we're trying to do business. Mr. Travers, my wife."

We smiled, made our little bows and said our how-d'you-dos.

"So sorry to interrupt you," she told me, "but there was something I had to tell my husband. I changed my mind about going straight to town, darling, so I rang Sylvia and I'm having tea with her and the children. I'll catch the three o'clock. Any messages you want to send?"

He'd been gently shepherding her towards the door.

"I don't think so. Give them my love. And your head-ache. It's better?"

"Absolutely gone."

She turned at the door and gave me a parting smile.

"Goodbye, Mr. Travers. I hope to see you again. And be sure to do a lot of business with my husband."

The door closed on them. There'd been a grim irony about that short farewell.

To me, of course, she was virtually a stranger but I'd thought she'd looked much older than when I'd seen her last. In spite of the make-up, the face had been too pale and the eyes too dark. I could just catch the faint voices beyond the door and then Morchard came back.

"Sorry about that. Why it had to happen this particular morning I don't know. She knows perfectly well what the procedure is. She'd only to ring me or ask at Enquiries."

"Maybe it's symptomatic," I said. "She forgot. She's all on edge."

"You may be right," he said, and waved me to the chair.

I said I'd have to be getting back to town. Now I knew that he still wished to employ us, I ought to be making plans. He rang through to his secretary, asked her to have the car ready, and said he'd be free in five minutes. He helped me on with my overcoat and walked with me across the lobby. He stopped just short of the passage.

"That business of my wife now knowing your name. I don't like it"

I smiled. "She's no idea where I'm from. She couldn't possibly trace me."

"I don't know," he said. "She has a whole lot at stake. And she has your description. She's a clever woman, Travers. Far cleverer than you'd think."

I made no comment and we moved on. He stopped again, this time just short of Enquiries.

"Just a moment. There's something I feel I ought to do."

He looked into the room, caught the receptionist's eye and beckoned. She came out. He smiled.

"Miss Allen. I want to ask you something highly confidential. When Mrs. Morchard came by just a few minutes ago, did she speak with you?"

She nervously moistened her lips. "Yes, sir. She wanted to know the name of the gentleman who was in your office."

He gave her another smile.

"I see. Tell me exactly what she said."

"Well, sir, she said did I know the name of the gentleman who was in your office, so I told her he was a Mr. Travers: a Mr. Ludovic Travers. Then she said did I know his business and I said no. Then she said had the gentleman come by chance or had you been expecting him and I said you'd expected him."

"I see." He turned to me. "That's spoiled everything. You see, Miss Allen, Mr. Travers and I were planning a pleasant surprise for Mrs. Morchard. Now we'll have to think of something else. By the way, this is not to be mentioned. Understood?"

We moved on to the main door.

"I don't like it," he said. "You remember what I was telling you about her being suspicious? She has your description and your full name."

I smiled.

"Very well. She can possibly find out, if she thinks it worth the trouble, that I run a detective agency. It may make her more careful. I think it's more likely to make her take a false step. She may get herself into a position where you can tell her you know something's wrong. In any case, don't worry. You're paying us to do that."

"God, how I hate it!" He held me for a moment by the arm. "All this damn subterfuge. Lying to my wife. Even lying to my staff. The whole thing's dirty. Disreputable. For God's sake do all you can. Money doesn't matter. Just find him."

"We'll do our best. We can't do more. If he's to be found, we'll find him."

I meant what I said. As we stood there I was suddenly feeling an enormous pity—and a liking.

"Better you than me," he said.

We'd been moving slowly towards the car where the driver stood waiting. Now he took my arm again.

"You know what I think I'd do if I found him? I'd strangle him with these two hands."

"And then?"

"I don't know. But no one would know it. He'd simply disappear from all our lives."

He stayed there while I moved on the few yards to the car. I glanced back as we went through the main gates and he was still standing there.

8
MARCH OF EVENTS

I LEFT the train at London Bridge. It had been a slow, and it was not far short of two o'clock. I'd breakfasted early and was feeling uncommonly hungry, so I rang the office and said I'd be in at half-past two.

"Mrs. Travers rang you," Bertha said. "Only a few minutes ago. I said you were away and she said would you ring her as soon as you came in."

Something about the evening's arrangements, I thought, and left it at that. I found a snack bar, had some sandwiches and coffee, and walked through to Broad Street. The other three were there. I should have told you, by the way, that it was a Tuesday.

I made a report. I'd actually passed The Cedars that morning—the driver had pointed it out to me—so I gave French his bearings for the morning. He would be using his own car, just in case. If Lydia Morchard took her usual train. Hallows would pick her up at Cannon Street. French would join him later at Welney House. There was plenty of parking space there.

I remembered something. I mentioned it to Hallows when French had gone. Norris had the first snuffles of a head cold and was thinking of going home early.

"Lydia's seeing her daughter this afternoon," I said. "She's coming up by the three o'clock from Sevenoaks, so if you'd like a little preliminary practice, you could pick her up."

We looked up the train. It was a non-stop from Sevenoaks to Charing Cross. I gave him Sylvia's address. I said that when I'd seen Lydia that morning she'd been wearing a two-piece—we used to call it a costume—in dark brown tweed and a matching hat. He said he'd take his car, just in case. We have an arrangement with a garage a few yards away in Hillyer Street.

As soon as he'd gone, I remembered Bernice and rang her. "The most curious thing happened," she told me. "A woman rang just before I rang Bertha and asked if you were in. I said you weren't, so she asked where she could get in touch with you and I gave her the number."

"Just a minute," I said. "What's so curious about that? Unless you suspect me of keeping two homes going."

"Don't be stupid," she told me crisply. "This is exactly what happened. I gave our number as usual and a woman's voice said 'Is that Mrs. Travers?' I said 'Yes' and she said 'Mrs. Ludovic Travers?', and I said 'Yes', and then she asked if you were in. I said you weren't and she asked where she could get in touch with you. What I thought afterwards was that if she'd wanted to consult you, she'd have known the Broad Street number already."

"You'd have thought so. What was her voice like?"

"Well, there wasn't very much of it. An educated voice. Very slow and distinct."

"Her age?"

"Betwixt and between. Someone of my age, perhaps."

"And you'd never heard it before?"

"Of course not, darling. If I had I'd have told you."

"Of course you would," I said. "She hasn't called me here. Perhaps she will later. Thanks for letting us know."

I knew it must have been Lydia Morchard. Almost as soon as she'd reached home, she'd checked the London directory and found a Travers, L. My name's listed only at the flat. Once she had the Broad Street number from Bernice it would have been easy to find out whose number it was. Then she could have double checked by calling us. If I'd actually been in, she'd have made some excuse and rung off.

What really worried me was why she'd regarded me as someone suspicious: inimical, that is, to what plans she'd been making with her son. Then something struck me. I've often said flippantly that I'm the sort of person who, seen once, is never forgotten. There's my height and the big horn-rims: the trim moustache and the occasionally unruly hair that gives me the look of a secretary bird. So when she'd seen me with her husband that morning, she'd asked herself where she'd seen me before. And she had seen me before. There'd been no more than a hundred people at that lecture I'd attended, and Bernice and I had been in the second row.

The question was, what effect would it have on any plans she'd already made. One thing was certain. She wouldn't let her husband know that the man he'd quoted as a prospective customer had been a private detective. It would make her all the more wary. If it came to that, it would make us more wary too.

I left it at that. Norris had decided to go home and I began finishing some of his work. Then at about a quarter-past five, Bertha buzzed through to say a lady was on the line. She wouldn't give her name. I asked her to put her through.

"Mr. Travers, this is Sylvia Fairfield. Something I think you ought to know. Mother came to see us this afternoon and she had a small suitcase with her. She said she'd intended to take it to her office before coming here, and then she'd changed her mind and would I mind keeping it for her. She said it had some important documents in it and then she came over all secretive, if you know what I mean. I had to promise I wouldn't mention the case to Harry."

"I see. And what'd you do with the case?"

"Put it under Susan's bed. We have a day Nannie, but I do the children's beds before she gets here. Do you think I did right? To tell you, I mean? I promised faithfully not to mention it to Harry but, of course, she knew nothing about you."

"You did very right," I told her. "Don't mention it to anyone else. Just keep it between you and me. It's safe where it is. By the way, anything said about how long you were to keep it?"

"Only a day or two. She said she'd be dropping in soon for lunch and take it then. She'd let me know."

"I see. And you realise what all this is about?"

"I think so. It's something to do with her and Lionel."

"And you're prepared to do anything to help your father and myself to stop anything disastrous happening?"

"Anything, Mr. Travers. Anything."

"Right," I said. "Just go on being your normal self, particularly with your husband. As soon as your mother lets you know when she's collecting that case, ring me here. If I'm not in, leave a message with the receptionist."

"I will," she said. "And thank you for everything."

"It's you who should be thanked," I said. "Kiss those lovely children of yours for me and go on being your charming self." I'd hardly put the receiver down when Hallows rang.

"I picked up the lady," he told me, "and luckily she took a taxi. She stayed with her daughter for over an hour and then she took the underground at South Kensington. I guessed she was making for home. Oh, and by the way, she had a small, brownish suitcase with her when she went into the flat but she hadn't it when she came out. Might have been returning it. Or presents for the children. Something like that. It certainly wasn't empty."

"Right. And now you're off home?"

He said he was. I said I'd like him to drop in at the office in the morning before going to Cannon Street.

*

The next morning—the Wednesday—I was early at the office. Hallows came in just before nine and I told him about Sylvia Fairfield. He gave a low whistle.

"Looks like things are hotting up. What d'you think's in that case?"

"One of two things, or both. It could possibly be something personal or it could be money. I'd say money. That's what Palling wants from his mother."

"But he *has* money. He can't have run through four thousand pounds?"

"Money's a thing you can always do with more of," I said. "But think back. Maybe you're not as conversant with things as I've been, but you do remember, if what happened at the Harringdon's anything to go by, that Palling's taken on a partner. Hitherto he's been strictly a lone wolf. If that means anything, it means he's planning a real killing. A sort of once and for all."

"Yes," he said. "A suitcase full of money. You think Mrs. Fairfield would let us have a look at it? It'd be easy."

"The way I see it, it's not vital," I said. "What happens to be in that case doesn't matter; it's what's done with it. And you and I know it's going to be handed over to Palling and that's our chance to collar him. We'll never get a better."

For once I was right. We left it that way and he went off to Cannon Street. And then Norris turned up. I cursed the daylights out of him for not being home in bed, but he said he'd had a few aspirins and a hot toddy the previous night and he thought he had the cold well beaten. It didn't look like it to me.

I settled down to some work of mine. At coffee time Bertha brought in some more mail and with it was a parcel. It was a stout, rectangular cardboard box about a foot by six inches. It had a West End postmark.

I looked up at Bertha and there must have been something curious on my face. She gave a tentative smile.

"You don't think it could be a bomb?"

I laughed. "Looks more like a bottle to me. We can soon see."

It *was* a bottle—a bottle of Irish whiskey. Written in ink on the label was, "Many, many thanks." The writing conveyed nothing to me. And then I had an idea. I thought I knew who'd sent it. Isabel Herne.

I don't care a lot for whiskey. Beer's my favourite drink. At home I take a strong whiskey when I'm mentally tired. With me it acts as a tonic, and I take it with soda. Irish whiskey I never take. I don't like the peaty flavour.

I was putting the bottle in a drawer when an idea came. I took it instead to Norris.

"A present just arrived," I told him. "I think it's from Isabel Herne. You take it. I've no use for it."

He looked at it. He gave an appreciative nod.

"Sure you don't want it?"

"Dead sure," I told him, and left it at that.

I went out to lunch as usual. At about half-past two Hallows rang. Lydia Morchard had taken her usual train and had spent the morning at her office. At about a quarter to two she had left and had taken the Underground from St. Paul's. She had got out at Bond Street and was now at the headquarters of the Home Protection League in Ashmore Street. It might be a long visit. French was with him.

I suggested the really important thing was still that suitcase, so if she went straight from Ashmore Street to her train, there'd be no need to report again. If anything should happen, that'd be different. He agreed.

By half-past three I was at a loose end, and then it suddenly occurred to me there was something I ought to do. Morchard had mentioned it and it might be as well to have an answer when we next met. What he'd obviously had in mind when he'd spoken of paying off the loan company was a placating of the police. It depended, of course, on whether the company was prepared to drop charges.

I took a bus to the Strand side of Covent Garden and walked through to Havelock Street. Hackle was in. I don't say he was all that friendly, but he warmed up as we went along. I had to go pretty cautiously. I'd unearthed a former friend, I said, who'd be prepared to do almost anything to save Gower from serious trouble. In fact, he was prepared to pay back the loan, together with expenses, provided all charges were dropped. Hackle put up a good show. He'd have to talk it over.

I smiled.

"Then talk it over. You don't have to be mysterious with me. Ring Maylock and put the proposition up to him."

He gave me a pained look, but he dialled the number. Two or three minutes and he replaced the receiver and I'd gathered what he'd been told to say.

"Yes, sir: we'll agree to that. You can tell us when payment is likely to be made?"

"I can't," I said. "All I can do is give you my personal word here and now that payment will definitely be made."

That, he said, was good enough.

"Perhaps it was a good thing after all that we didn't catch up with him at that hotel," he said. "This way everything'll be settled and no bones broken—so to speak. You'd like a cup of tea? I was just about to have one myself."

"Thank you, no," I said. "I think I'll just have a word with Hewes and then be getting along."

He frowned. "If it's about telling him that the search is being called off, then I think I'd better tell him myself. In any case he isn't in. He's having some temporary trouble at home."

"Not wife trouble?" I'd forgotten momentarily that Hewes had spoken of himself as a widower.

"Oh, no. His wife died—oh, must be twenty years ago. He ought to be in tomorrow, though, if you really wanted to see him."

"I don't," I said. "As I was here, I thought of just putting my head round the door. Just a word. I haven't seen him since that Harringdon business. I suppose he took it pretty badly?"

"Yes," he said. "Still, everything's been pretty bad lately. I don't think he'll carry on much longer. Not a nice prospect to have to fend for yourself. I've seen it coming."

"Old and disillusioned?"

"I don't know that you aren't right. His health hasn't been too good, you know. He'll have his pension, of course, and he ought to have something put away."

"Who'll take over? Peplow?"

"Don't know," he said. "He's certainly a more energetic type than Hewes. And, between ourselves, he could make a better hand of the job. Whether he could afford to buy the business remains to be seen. Everything's very much in the air."

He went with me to the door. As we shook hands he asked me if I'd like to leave any message for Hewes. I told him not to bother. Now the search for the elusive

Gower was being called off, I didn't suppose we'd ever run across each other again.

I stood for a moment by the kerb in Havelock Street and suddenly I felt like having a cup of tea. Not that I was sorry to have refused Hackle's offer. At any rate I walked back to the Strand, and it was around half-past four when I took a Liverpool Street bus.

Bertha had been waiting for me. I'd only just stepped inside the door when she was opening her own. She was all of a fluster.

"Oh, Mr. Travers, I'm glad you've come. Mr. Norris has had an attack of some kind. He still looks frightfully ill."

"You called the doctor?"

"No, sir: he wouldn't let me. He said he'd be all right."

I hurried through to Norris's room. He was lying back in the easy chair and the electric fire was on. He looked ghastly.

"It's all right," he said. "Nothing to worry about."

"Don't talk damn nonsense," I told him. "You look like nothing on earth. What was it? Not your heart?"

He smiled. "My heart's all right. All it was was being damn near poisoned."

"Poisoned! What was it? Something you ate?"

"Something I drank," he said. "That Irish whiskey."

I stared.

"Look," he said. "Stop fussing. And shut that door in case Bertha comes in. It was just a nasty shock, that's all."

He began telling me about it. It wasn't like him, he said, to feel tired, but at four o'clock, when Bertha usually brought in tea, he'd felt like something stronger, so he'd asked her to slip out and buy a lemon and bring it in with the sugar and the boiling kettle. It was about five minutes before she was back and, as he'd realised he'd have to hold the fort in her room, he mixed the toddy there. He took it to his office, and what saved him was the fact that it was too hot to drink.

He hadn't thought of that. He'd burnt his mouth and, at the very first second of taste, he'd been aware of an extraordinary bitterness and he'd spat the whole thing out. He'd put his fingers down his throat and tried to be sick, and it was the retching that had made him feel queer. That, and the shock of discovery.

He'd thought at first that Bertha had somehow put salt instead of sugar in the bowl. Then he'd gingerly tasted another drop of the toddy and he knew. That whiskey had been poisoned. He'd put a drop of it on his tongue and was dead sure. Then he'd asked Bertha to bring in some tea after all. He couldn't have been looking too good and, for want of a better excuse, had told her he'd had an attack of coughing.

The bottle and the almost cold toddy were in the cupboard. Before I took out the cork I had a good look at it through the big glass. It was one of those modern corks that don't need a corkscrew, and I thought I could just discern a minute perforation through its plastic top, but I couldn't be sure.

I put a drop of the whiskey on my tongue. There was no doubt about the bitterness.

"I think you're right about poison," I said. "It's no consolation, I know, but this was meant for me."

Bertha buzzed through to say Hallows was on the line. All he wanted was to report that Lydia Morchard had gone home early. She'd just taken a train from Charing Cross. I asked him to get along to the office. Something important had turned up.

"You think you can hold the fort till Bob gets back?" I asked Norris.

"Look," he said. "There's nothing wrong with me now. It was just the shock, that's all."

"All the same, you'd better take a taxi home," I said. "I'm taking this bottle to the Yard."

He stared. "I thought we agreed not to bring them into it."

"I'm not," I said. "I'm going to be the most ignorant person alive. By the way, why should you think it's connected with the Morchard case?"

"What else could it be?"

I shrugged my shoulders. I said maybe he was right.

I rang Jewle from my room and he happened to be in. I said something important had turned up and I had to see him at once. Before he could start too much probing, I rang off.

Another twenty minutes and I was in his room. That young sergeant who'd been with Matthews at the Harringdon was there.

"What's all this?" Jewle said, as I put down my parcel.

"A bottle of Irish whiskey," I said, "and the wrappings it came in. Someone tried to poison me."

He thought for a moment I was joking. He changed his mind when he saw the actual bottle. He was just about to lift it.

"What about prints?"

"I don't think they matter. It's smothered with them in any case. Whoever was clever enough to plan the poisoning would have been careful about prints."

He had a look at the cork. I told him I'd thought there was a perforation but I couldn't be sure.

"You mean the syringe trick? Drawing out some whiskey and pushing in some poison?"

"Something like that."

He sniffed the bottle. He tried a drop and made a grimace. "Something there that shouldn't be. You'd like us to check it?"

The sergeant left with the parcel. Jewle told me to make myself at home. He took out his pipe and I took out mine.

"You may have had a lucky escape," he said. "How come you didn't actually drink the stuff?"

I told him the whole story from the very beginning. "Tough luck on Norris," he said. "And you thought the bottle was a present from a grateful client."

"I did. On the label, as you may have seen, was, 'Many, many thanks'."

"And who do you think it really came from?"

"Heaven knows," I said. "Strange as it may seem to you, I don't think I have any enemies."

"And what about that so-called Gower? You're still looking for him?"

"Why should I? You people are doing that. As far as my client's concerned, everything was settled days ago. In fact I'm now prepared to tell you her name. In confidence, of course."

"We might just want it later. And you really haven't an idea who was behind this business?"

"I just told you so."

"So you did."

He was smiling slightly as he got his pipe going.

"Well, we'll have to try to get to the bottom of it. Things wouldn't be the same here if you weren't popping in and out."

"I'm grateful," I said. "Thank you, Monsieur le Duc de la Rochefoucauld."

He stared. "Sorry. I didn't catch that."

"Just thinking aloud," I said. "He was a Frenchman. Used to spend a lot of his time making epigrams. There was one about there being always something in the misfortunes of our friends that isn't wholly displeasing to us."

He's none too quick a thinker but he gets there.

"My dear fellow, you can't think—"

The buzzer went. He picked up the receiver. A very few seconds and he was putting it back. He wasn't smiling.

"You were right. There was a perforation in that bottle. The poison was strychnine."

I didn't speak. I was thinking of Norris.

"It's still far too easy to get hold of. Rat poisons and that sort of thing. Luckily someone grossly over-estimated the dose. Wanted to make sure, perhaps. That tell you anything?"

"Only that if that toddy hadn't been so hot, Norris might have taken a good swig at it."

"Yes," he said. "But what it tells me is that it was the work of a raw amateur. Someone in a hurry. In fact, your friend Gower. You practically nabbed him at the Harringdon. I think whoever rang him there gave him the tip you were on his heels. That's why he made up his mind to get you out of the way once and for all."

I must have looked staggered. There were more holes in that theory than you'd find in a colander. Luckily he took the look for the dawn of revelation.

"You agree?"

"Maybe I do."

"Right," he said. "It'll be tough going but we'll do our best. You got anything to suggest?"

I said I hadn't, and he got to his feet. "If anything happens we'll let you know at once."

He helped me on with my overcoat. As we went towards the door, his hand fell on my shoulder.

"Give my regards to Norris. And about that Frenchman. I think he was just a smart Aleck."

It was late, but something told me to go back to the office. The night-duty man was in Bertha's room, and he told me Hallows was still there. I found him in that cubby-hole of his just off Norris's office. He's very rarely in and he reckons that room's big enough.

"Thought I'd wait and hear what'd happened," he said. "Norris is a lot better. I let him go home under his own steam."

I told him what had happened at the Yard. Jewle, I said, had had a few of the right ideas and, luckily for us, had put them wrongly together. My idea was that Matthews was handling things and what Jewle knew was largely from hearsay. In any case we were safe enough so far. The original case and the Morchard one could go on being entirely different things.

"You think Palling sent that bottle?"

"Who else?" I said. "Look at the sequence. His mother's in touch with him. Yesterday morning she discovered who I was. That suitcase business shows things are coming to a head. She was almost certainly in touch with him and warned him about me, so he took his own measures to make sure I didn't interfere."

"I think you're right," he said. "Things are really coming to a head. Something's got to happen pretty quick. Maybe tomorrow."

9
SUITCASE

NORRIS turned up the next morning at his usual time and looking almost his normal self. He may be well over sixty but he likes to show us comparative weaklings what fitness can do. When I asked what his doctor had said, he gave a look of pained reproach. All he'd swallowed of that dope, he said, wouldn't have floated a flea. All that was left of the experience was a slight tickling of the throat.

I thought there was just a touch of bravado in the way he went off to his office. Bob Hallows was in a few minutes later. Just before ten o'clock French rang to say Lydia Morchard hadn't stirred from the house. Her husband had left in his Humber just before nine.

It was only about ten minutes later when Sylvia Fairfield rang.

"Mother has changed her mind," she told me. "She's just rung to say she can't come to lunch after all, but she's coming to tea. And she mentioned that—you know what, under Susan's bed. She said she doesn't want it in town after all and she's taking it home with her."

I thanked her warmly.

"Just behave perfectly normally. And don't show any special interest in that suitcase. We'll do the rest."

I heard her let out a breath.

"I feel awfully guilty about this. Somehow it all seems so underhand. I don't mean you: I mean me."

"That's because you don't know what's at stake," I said. "I hoped I wouldn't have to tell you this but your brother's got a whole string of new crimes to answer for. The police want him pretty badly and what we want to do is get to him before they do. It's the only way to avoid a dreadful scandal."

"I'm sorry," she said. "I didn't know that. Is there anything else I can do?"

"Just do as I suggested and act perfectly normally. If you were to ring me after your mother leaves, I'd be grateful."

There was nothing else from French, which meant that Lydia was still at home. By one o'clock it looked as if she wouldn't be leaving till just in time for that afternoon train she'd taken before. It isn't often at Broad Street that there's any tension in the air, but there definitely was that afternoon. We like to do a job well. But we're not philanthropists and quite a lot of money was at stake.

When French rang to say that Lydia had taken that through train to Charing Cross, it was a relief to have some action. French said, too, that she was wearing a black costume with a reddish scarf and a black hat with some red trimmings. He would join Hallows, as arranged, near Stanwick House.

Hallows left at once to fetch his car. I had a long wait ahead, and I couldn't help cursing the bad luck that led to Lydia Morchard's recognising me. But for that I'd certainly have been with Hallows in his car, with Norris at the end of a telephone instead of myself. All the time, too, I kept wondering where the chase would lead, and in what corner of town our man would be holed up. At least we'd been right in our guess about one thing. That night flight to Victoria from the Harringdon Hotel had definitely been a blind. Not that we'd shown any peculiar perspicacity. Even Hewes had made the same guess.

I was at my desk with little to do but think and all the time in the world, and that's why that sudden remembrance of Hewes, and the call on Hackle the previous afternoon, kept my thoughts in the same direction. I'd liked Hewes. I'd definitely enjoyed that half-hour I'd spent in his office, and I couldn't help wondering what those domestic troubles were.

Not, I smugly told myself, that they'd be the only causes of his parting with his business.

Once, in his heavy, cautious way, he'd probably been something of a go-getter. Then he'd slowly relapsed into little more than a telephone watcher, with Peplow doing the leg-work. A kind of slow deterioration. That was why that call of mine had given him so much pleasure. It had been a rare break in a deadly monotony. But Peplow: there was something different. He'd struck me as quite a good man. If he wasn't acquiring Hewes's business, we might find something for him ourselves. Hewes had lost his touch. If Peplow had been in charge of that Harringdon business and not Hewes things might have been vastly different.

There was a tap at the door. Bertha was bringing in tea. I looked up at the clock. Half-past four already. If things went the way they'd done before, Lydia should be leaving her daughter's flat in just over half an hour. It might be quite a time, of course, before I heard from Hallows.

It was just a quarter-past five when Sylvia rang. Her mother had just left, and she'd taken the suitcase. She was going to South Kensington Station. When she got to Leicester Square, she'd walk the few yards to Charing Cross.

"The suitcase," I said. "Was it heavy or light?"

"I don't know," she said. "I think it was fairly light. Mother carried it quite comfortably. She wouldn't let me take it."

"And how was she? Nervy at all?"

"Not mother," she said. "She can carry anything off. I did think she was a bit chatty. And I did catch her looking at her watch."

I thanked her. If anything happened I'd let her know at once.

I settled down to some more waiting. Norris came in to hear the latest developments, then left for home. I'd be waiting till Hallows let me know where he and French were holding Palling, and then I'd join them. The night-duty man would arrive at six. If I'd already left, Bertha would have stayed on.

I began to think about that suitcase. What I thought wasn't as logical as this, but it boiled itself down to the space required for banknotes. We keep a certain amount of money in the safe, just in case, and you'd be surprised at the number and variety of our gadgets: at any rate I weighed a packet of a hundred pound-notes on the scales, made some measurements and did some calculations.

How much money would Palling have demanded? If he had to share the big killing with a confederate, then maybe as much as ten thousand pounds. And it's amazing how small a space that amount in pound-notes can occupy. A suitcase of the kind Sylvia Fairfield had described could easily hold it, and the weight wouldn't be beyond a woman's power to carry with no great strain. If the amount were in fivers, the less the space and weight. A man with enough and sufficiently large pockets could easily bestow the whole amount about his person. In other words, if Palling could empty that case, he'd have no case to carry. I wondered if Hallows had thought about that.

Just as I looked up at the clock—it was only a quarter-to six—the buzzer went. Hallows was on the line.

"Yes, Bob? Where're you speaking from?"

"Charing Cross Station. I've just seen the lady leave for home."

"You mean she's still got the case with her!"

"No," he said. "The whole thing's been the most inglorious bitch-up. I'll get back at once and tell you about it. By the way, French is on that train to see she really goes straight home."

He rang off. I just sat there. What the devil had gone wrong I couldn't imagine. If a certain sanity hadn't returned, I'd probably have worked myself up into quite a pitch of anger. Even so, I just couldn't believe it. That Hallows should have been somehow outwitted by Lydia Morchard was unthinkable. I began prowling about the room. I told Bertha she could go home. I wondered what in Heaven's name we were going to tell Henry Morchard. If its author needed inspiration, he could have taken one look at me and settled down to a sequel to *Cat On A Hot Tin Roof*.

And then at last Hallows came in. He was his usual unruffled self.

"Sorry about all this. Nobody's fault really. The only thing to blame was the rush hour. Everything had been too well timed. We never had a chance."

He looked a bit tired. I poured him a sherry and had one myself.

"Just what happened exactly?"

"I'll tell you," he said. "Everything went perfectly. We picked her up and followed her the short distance to South Kensington Station. I'd already arranged about parking the car. She bought her ticket but she didn't go downstairs: just hung about as if she was waiting for someone. And looking at the dock. Then she went down.

Soon as she was on the platform, we split up: one each side of her, just a few yards away. You can guess what that platform was like at the rush hour. Absolutely chock-a-block. When the train came in there was the usual surge forward. We'd arranged to take the doors each side of her and close in a bit nearer as soon as the train moved off. The last I saw of her, she was still holding the suitcase and trying to make a way through to the middle door. We squeezed in at the two side doors. A few people got out at Sloane Square and she managed to get a seat. That's when I noticed it. 'My God!' I said to myself. 'What the hell's happened to that suitcase?'"

"She hadn't got it?"

"Not a sign of it. Both French and I got up close at Hyde Park Corner and there she was sitting. Devil a sign of the case. When she got out at Leicester Square she just walked unconcernedly to the escalator, and all she was carrying was a little black-and-white handbag."

"Yes," I said slowly. "She had the case when she made for the doors. In the rush someone relieved her of it, as arranged. All he had to do was stay on the platform and then make his way up."

"That's it," he said. "And French and I'd be on the way to Sloane Square like a couple of fools."

"You don't think she spotted you?"

He snorted. "Utterly impossible. What we couldn't know was that the whole thing'd be timed as it was. I'd say that Palling himself tapped her on the shoulder in that rush for the doors, whispered something, and took the case. That's how it was arranged. And if you can tell me how we could have anticipated it, I'd like to hear it."

"We couldn't," I said. "We were just outsmarted. By the way, you didn't see anyone on the platform who might have been taken for Palling?"

"Never a hope," he said. "What I can say is that we saw no one approach her the minute or so before the train came in. After that we had our hands full. Everyone else only had to get on that train. We had to try to keep an eye on her as well."

"Ah well," I said resignedly. "It's spilt milk and there's no use crying. We were just outsmarted. What I'm thinking about now is what we ought to say to Henry Morchard."

"I've been thinking about that too," he said. "You know what I think we should tell him? Just nothing."

"You mean write it off and try again? If so, how are we going to get another chance?"

"It wasn't that. The way I've been seeing it is this. She's been pestered for money. Some kind of blackmail. She stuck it out for a time and then gave in. It's worried her like hell. Agreed?"

"Agreed."

"Right," he said. "Then why not do this? Wait a couple of days or so and then have a confidential word with the client. Ask him if any change has come over his wife. Is the tension less. If it definitely is, then we tell him just what's been happening. Then we can really put the screws on."

"Don't get you," I said. "Who's going to put the screws on whom?"

He told me. The more he told me, the more I liked it. Maybe, I said, that afternoon's fiasco had been all to the good. If Morchard could screw courage to the sticking point—and I believed he could—then the whole case might be cleared up in no time. There was just one thing I

wanted avoided. Sylvia Fairfield was far too nice a person
to be any further involved.

So things were to be left in abeyance till the Monday
morning, when we'd get into touch with Morchard. My
job was to work out the plan of campaign. That suitcase
was going to be the tricky point, and the morning after
that latest fiasco I knew I'd have to see Sylvia again. She'd
be wondering in any case why I hadn't kept the promise
to give her the news.

So I rang her. I said I'd rather tell her personally what
had happened the previous afternoon than talk about
it over the telephone. She said she'd be in. Nannie had
taken Susan for her usual walk in Kensington Gardens
and David was at school. Twenty minutes later I was
ringing the bell of the flat.

There was a difference from my last visit: the absence
of people that makes a strange emptiness. She had coffee
ready and we sat in the same handsome lounge. This
time the curtains of the tall windows were drawn back
and you could see the green of trees.

"Things didn't go so well last night," I said. "Your
brother managed to collect that suitcase from your mother
without being seen."

She actually smiled. "But isn't that good? I mean she's
got rid of him. Now we can be ourselves again."

"Oh, no," I told her. "What your mother's done is just
the opposite. Yesterday afternoon was our great chance
to catch up with him before the police do. Every police
force in the country knows about your brother and it's
only a matter of time. Even if he's gone abroad with the
money your mother's given him, Interpol will catch up
with him. They may have him tomorrow: next week, next

month, but they'll have him. You may think me brutal but all your mother has done is finance a criminal. When the money's gone she'll either have to find more or he'll start that career of his all over again."

Her eyes puckered with pain.

"All the same there's a bright side to it," I said. "We're now in a position to confront your mother with certain facts. The most damning one will be that suitcase."

There was a sudden alarm.

"No, no," I said. "You won't come into it at all. Your mother isn't the only one who can concoct fairy-tales. Tell me: when is this flat absolutely empty?"

"Generally of a morning. This morning I had things to do. Also I thought you might ring, or I'd have gone with Nannie and Susan to the Gardens."

"Right," I said. "Then the morning after your mother left that suitcase here, someone made an entry here and opened it and had a look at what was in it. That's purely hypothetical of course."

"Oh!" She smiled relievedly. "I thought you were really serious."

"I am," I said, "in a hypothetical way. We're very careful workers when we do a job of that kind, so naturally you never had the least suspicion. That leaves you out. Mind if I have a look at where the case was put?"

That quite large nursery had probably been converted from a dining-room. Besides the little twin beds there were toys, a train set, a couple of decorated cupboards and even murals.

I had a good look round.

"Your mother's a very clever woman," I said. "She'll almost certainly try to call my bluff. I've got to be able to tell her just what was seen when we looked in that case. This one's Susan's bed, if I remember right."

I had a good look at it. I even got down on my knees and looked under it. And that was about all. I reassured her again as we stood for a minute at the outer door.

"There'll be no possible chance of connecting you with any of this. You've been a great help. Thanks to you, everything ought to be cleared up very early next week."

There was no more action till early on the Monday morning, and then I called Morchard at the plant. I had to wait a minute or two while his secretary located him.

"Yes?" he said. I hadn't given the secretary my name.

"Travers," I said. "There have been some very serious developments, but before I get on to that I must ask you a question. It's not a frivolous one. I want you to think back to last Thursday night and tell me whether there's been any change in your wife during the period from then till now. Less tension, for example."

"Yes," he said. "There's been a considerable change. She's practically her usual self. I'd even thought of ringing you to ask if you could suggest any connection. She was in her constituency all Saturday and she came home feeling quite optimistic about even that."

I guessed he'd be a mighty hard man to scare but I had to have a try. What he'd told me, I said, merely confirmed that things were worse than I'd thought. I kept talking in case he should butt in. Not that things were desperate. Provided he gave us an absolutely free hand, I thought the whole thing could be cleared up in a couple of days. His full co-operation would be needed. I almost reinforced it with a cliché about the moment of truth, but some remnant of discrimination made me put it another way. Since Hemingway wrote *Death in the Afternoon*, that little four-word gem has long since become costume jewellery.

"You've got me bewildered," he said. "Just what is it you want to do? And me to do."

I said that Hallows, a partner of mine, had been associated with me on the case. He and I wanted to come down to Sevenoaks the next morning. We'd arrive at about a quarter to nine. He would still be in the house and so, of course, would his wife. I wanted her to be suddenly confronted with us. All he'd have to do was admit employing us, and why. We'd take it from then on.

He thought for a moment. "You think such a course is absolutely necessary?"

"Either that, or you confront your wife with certain facts we'll give you, and decide if you want us to continue. I think we ought to be there. We know all the facts."

"What facts?"

"That on Thursday afternoon last she gave her son a considerable sum of money. We weren't in a position to hold him."

I heard him let out a sigh. When he spoke I was surprised at the sharpness in his tone. "This is once and for all. It can't be allowed to go on. Come down as you suggest."

"One thing I want to assure you," I said. "There'll be no brow-beating. It's just that in our opinion your wife should be told that you're aware of what she's done. She may know Lionel's whereabouts and decide to let us handle things your way."

"You're right," he said. "I never doubted your handling the thing tactfully."

A minute or two and we'd made arrangements about the morning. It had been a tricky business. Maybe I could have blabbered a little less and have come sooner to the point. I just didn't know. I'm not being trite when I say that husband and wife are a unique relationship. We don't handle divorce cases. Intrinsically they're different. There you have parties who are estranged or likely to be so. Morchard and his wife, on the other hand, were a happily married couple. If someone came to me and said Bernice was a kleptomaniac, I'd be furious to say the least. If he proceeded to prove it, I'd still be resentful. Unreasonable, perhaps, but that's just how it would be. It's something inherent in a particular relationship. And that's why we'd gone so carefully into the way Morchard should be handled. There was still about it a trace of smugness that I didn't like, but it seemed the best we could do.

In the morning I was up very early. I picked up Hallows at South Norwood and headed east below Bromley and so to the Sevenoaks road. It was just comfortably short of the agreed time when we parked the car in the quiet road a little distance from the house.

It was a late Georgian house of two storeys, with a handsome door and fanlight, tall windows and a steepish, slated roof. The two trees from which it had had its name were well away to the back and we could just see their tops. From the circular, asphalted drive a side road went at a tangent to the left of the house: presumably to a garage. It skirted the French windows which Morchard had mentioned.

He'd opened them as arranged. We went through to what might once have been called a breakfast-room. A door to the far right opened into the drawing-room.

You could call it only that. Everything about it had quality. A washed Chinese carpet almost covered the floor.

There were a couple of handsome chandeliers and the whole room was a collector's dream. There was a superb Stubbs above the marble mantelpiece. Two magnificent satinwood cabinets had between them a long-cased clock that looked like a Tompion. That was all I had time to see. Morchard was coming through a door to our left. We shook hands and I introduced Hallows. Morchard gave me a shrewd look.

"I'll fetch Mrs. Morchard straight away," he told us. "She's looking over her correspondence in the library. I suppose I ought to be looking forward to this but—well. I just don't know. I'll go through with it, of course."

"I don't think you'll regret it," I told him. "I assure you we'll handle things with all possible tact."

He nodded as he turned away. A moment or two and my collector's eyes were going round that room again.

"A nice place," Hallows said, and gave a dry smile. "Doesn't look as if we'll have to worry about the bill."

I asked what he'd thought of Morchard.

"Looks as if he has a mind of his own. He'll carry it through all right."

The door opened again and Lydia Morchard came through. Her husband was just behind her. She gave a little start at the sight of me, then the look shifted to Hallows.

"I thought it better you shouldn't know who our two callers were," Morchard said. "You know Mr. Travers. This is his partner, Mr. Hallows."

In a way you couldn't help admiring her. There was something almost flirtatious in the way she looked round at her husband.

"But isn't Mr. Travers a customer of yours? I mean—well, what am I supposed to do?" She smiled. "Not to help to put over some deal?"

"Sit down, my dear," he told her gently. "And you too, gentlemen. I thought this would surprise you. Or perhaps it hasn't. I think you know that these gentlemen are private detectives. I hired them to protect you against yourself. To stop you ruining a whole family. I did it only when I was sure Lionel was back in England and you were in touch with him."

"But this is preposterous!" She'd have got to her feet if his hand hadn't held her back. "I'll never forgive you for this, Henry. You must be utterly mad!"

She was putting on quite a tantrum. I cut in with a placatory smile. "Mrs. Morchard, aren't you protesting too much? If you hadn't been in touch with your son, you'd have pointed out that you couldn't have communicated with him except by letter or cable. But you didn't even mention Australia where he's supposed to be. Besides, we know."

She made as if to get to her feet again. I had an idea that sheer curiosity would be the one thing that would keep her there.

"I absolutely refuse to listen."

"As you wish," I said. "If you don't listen, then I assure you that the moment you leave this room, I shall call Scotland Yard. You've been harbouring a criminal—"

She shook with anger. "How dare you! *My* son isn't a criminal."

Hallows came in. "Mrs. Morchard, what I'm going to tell you is the truth. If you don't believe it, you have only to pick up a telephone receiver and dial 999. Your son arrived back in England some three or four months ago. Since then he's committed thefts at two hotels, swindled a client of ours out of a great deal of money and robbed a loan company of five hundred pounds. The police have his fingerprints and there isn't a police force in the country that isn't on the look out for him. But for you, we might have found him. Your husband could have seen him. You thought you were avoiding a scandal. What you did was make it almost a certainty."

She'd been shaken but only for a moment. "It's utter and absolute nonsense. If you believe it, Henry, you must be mad!"

"But we've proof," Hallows said. "Undeniable proof. To start with, there's the suitcase."

She stared. "Suitcase? What suitcase?"

"You're making it very hard for us," I said. "You had to be kept under observation and for the simple reason that you might lead us to your son. We saw you enter your daughter's flat with a suitcase and leave later without it. We were suspicious. We wanted to know what was in that case, so when the flat was temporarily empty, we made an entry. We found that suitcase under a child's bed and it was easy enough to open it. You know what was in it . . ."

Once or twice her hand had gone almost wearily to her head. Suddenly she gave a little moan and slumped sideways in the chair. She'd have slithered to the ground if I hadn't held her.

"Oh, my God!" That was Morchard. "Stay here. I'll get some water."

I held him back.

"Better lay her on that settee. She'll come round in a minute or two. Water'll do no good."

We lifted her to the settee. I took Morchard by the arm and drew him a little way aside.

10

END OF AN EPISODE

What I said was within earshot of his wife. I wanted it to be. I was watching her. He had his back to her.

"A woman fainted in my office one day last year," I said. "And I sent for a doctor. After she'd recovered and we'd seen her into a taxi, he gave me a very queer look. He said a man of my experience ought to have known the difference between a sham faint and a real one. He told me how to detect it. It's an infallible test: just the extreme pallor of the face before the attack."

Lydia hadn't stirred. I knew I'd defeat my own ends if I didn't draw him farther away.

"You see, the pallor is a symptom of the faint, not an aftereffect. Your wife isn't pale, even now. In my opinion she threw that faint because she didn't want you to hear about that suitcase."

"You're sure?"

"Absolutely sure. She'll stage a recovery when it suits her, and if we leave you with her it ought to facilitate matters. You play up to her—so far. If she wants her doctor, tell him beforehand what you suspect. When he's gone, do some straight talking. Either a full confession or you ring Scotland Yard. You daren't risk trouble with the police. The threat's got to carry absolute conviction."

"I'll do it," he said. "We've got so far. Now it's got to be finished."

I beckoned Hallows over. "We'll go to the Angel and have coffee. If necessary, we'll have lunch. You ring us when she's ready to talk. If she still holds out ring us in her presence and instruct us to get in touch with the Yard."

"I'll do that," he told us. "Or there may be another way. We'll see."

We left by the way we'd come, turned back to the car and drove on to the Angel. We parked the car in the yard, bought a selection of newspapers at a newsagent's across the street and made our way to the hotel lounge. We ordered coffee and said we might be staying to lunch. The coffee came and we took our ease. It was only just half-past ten.

I glanced through a paper or two, then settled down to *The Times* crossword. Hallows, who's also something of an addict, was tackling another. Ten minutes went by and then, for the first time, one of us mentioned the case.

"I've been thinking," Hallows said. "There's another screw Morchard could put on if he knew about it. I mean that attempt at poisoning. She was responsible for that. Indirectly, but responsible."

I said it was an idea but we'd keep it in reserve. He didn't ask for reasons and I don't think I'd have told him if he had. But it's always seemed to me that all of us—dukes or dustmen—have one thing in common: a sense of our own dignity: the thing we sometimes call a personal importance or self-respect. Take that away from a man: smear it, injure it or go so far as to destroy it, and you've committed a despicable crime. We weren't out to lower Lydia Morchard in her husband's eyes. All we wanted to do was to put on enough pressure to make her talk. That couple would have to go on living together. What we thought about either was immaterial: what mattered was what they'd think about each other. If, as a last desperate resort, that threat had to be used, then I'd be the one to make it. Morchard himself would never know.

Noon came and the time for a tankard in the bar. We had lunch and went back to the lounge again to spin out the time over coffee. It was two o'clock when I was called to the phone.

"If you come in about half an hour's time, I think Lydia will be ready to talk," Morchard said. "She didn't want to face you people again, but I was sure you'd go easy with her."

"We will," I said. "You had to put on pressure?"

"Yes," he said. "Pressure of my own. You're not to give even a hint that you know of it, but I threatened to leave her." He hung up. I stood for a moment with the receiver in my hand. I don't know how I felt. Maybe it was a bit humble: the vague knowledge that Henry Morchard was a far better man than myself.

This time we went through the front door. An elderly maid showed us into the drawing-room. In a couple of minutes Morchard joined us. He had his wife affection-ately by the arm. The black skirt and white blouse of the morning had been changed for a reddish-coloured frock. Her cheeks were pale and the eyes dark. Maybe I was uncharitable but it mightn't have been wholly uncon-nected with make-up. I'd expected resentment or even hostility, but when our eyes met she actually gave a little smile of recognition.

"My wife has quite recovered now," Morchard told us. "This morning she was under far too great a strain. I'm sure you realised that."

"We do," I said. "Mrs. Morchard found herself placed in a virtually impossible position. May I assure you, Mrs. Morchard, that whatever you tell us now will be treated as very strictly confidential."

She sat very upright in the chair, hands folded almost demurely in her lap. I'm suspicious, as I said. I wondered what script she'd been writing for us. It certainly had a dramatic enough opening.

"I'm a mother . . . . Then suddenly I found myself involved in a conflict of interests and it was something I had to deal with alone. Perhaps that excuses what I did do. You can't reduce everything to logic."

"I know." I said. "Believe me, we do appreciate that."

"Thank you," she said quietly. "And there's something else that made a great difference. Until you told me about them this morning, I had no idea what dreadful things Lionel had been doing. What I was trying to do was protect him from the consequences of having broken his word and come home. I mean when he first rang me."

"And that was when?"

"About a fortnight ago. No one will ever know the shock it was to me. He said he was in trouble and would I let him have some money. I asked him what trouble, but he said he daren't tell me. I asked him where he was but he wouldn't tell me that either, so I absolutely refused to help. I did say I'd pay his passage back to Australia if he left at once. I also said no one would ever know he'd broken his word. He tried to start an argument but I rang off. I knew him so well. I knew if I listened to him I'd be cajoled into doing almost anything.

"Then he called again. About ten days ago. He said he was so desperate that he'd have to tell me after all just what trouble he was in. It was such an extraordinary story that I couldn't believe it. He said he'd had an English friend in Sydney whose brother in England knew something about a proposed train robbery, and advised him to come over. That, of course, was over a year ago, before anyone had even thought of that Big Train Robbery. At any rate, Lionel said they came here and got into what he called the organisation.

"That's why he and his friend, he said, were now liable at any moment to arrest and why they hadn't any money. They'd been concerned with the general planning and hadn't taken part in the operation. That's why they hadn't been at that farm when some of the robbery money was handed out; and immediately after that, of course, the gang was disturbed and had to disperse. All the money they'd had was two hundred pounds given them by one of the gang who'd later been picked up by the police. He said he and his friend had got down to virtually nothing and then a few days ago they'd made a connection with a freighter sailing for Quebec in about a week's time. If I'd let him have, say ten thousand pounds so that he and his friend could establish themselves over there, then he'd solemnly swear never to set foot here again."

"You believed him?"

"No," she said. "Not then. Even when he began imploring me to help him. I told him frankly I didn't believe him. I reminded him how many times he'd lied to me before. The following morning he rang again and he wanted me to listen to that friend of his. He said his name was Brown. He and that man really frightened me. I'll never forget the very words he said. 'Lady, what kind of a mother are you? You don't deserve to have a son like Lionel.'"

"What was his voice like?"

"It's difficult to say. There was definitely some Cockney in it. He sounded a much older man than Lionel. It was a quiet, stifled sort of voice. As if he was talking out of the corner of his mouth, like a gangster."

"And he frightened you?"

"He frightened me terribly. He said he and Lionel weren't going to lose their big chance to get away, so unless I wanted any trouble—big trouble, he said—I'd better do as Lionel said. I said I couldn't raise that amount of money. Even if I could, it would cause suspicions. Then just before he rang off, he said something that really frightened me. He asked if I loved my grandchildren."

"I see. Naturally you were frightened. I'd have been frightened myself. Did he make any other threats?"

"Only that I had twenty-four hours in which to make up my mind. It was after he'd hung up that I began to believe what Lionel had told me about the train robbery, so when Lionel called me the next morning I said I could just manage eight thousand pounds, but no more. It would take me two days to arrange it with the bank, so he said he'd call me again in two days' time. He said he was going to have a job trying to convince his friend Brown."

"I know," I said. "Trying to make sure you toed the line. And naturally you did get the money."

"May I interrupt?" That was Hallows. "Going back to this man Brown. Could he possibly have been non-existent? I mean, could the voice have been your son's?"

It was something that hadn't even occurred to her. She had to think.

"No," she said. "It couldn't have been Lionel. He couldn't possibly have changed his voice like that."

"Sorry to have interrupted. You were telling us about the money."

"Yes, the money. I made an arrangement with my bank. It was awkward having to explain such an amount in cash, but I said it was in connection with a charitable organisation in which I was interested. Everyone seemed to take it for granted. Then Lionel called me again to make sure

I had the money. He said I was to put it in a suitcase that evening after dark and leave it under the wall just inside the drive gate. I absolutely refused. There was quite an argument but I insisted. I said this was one place I was going to keep—well, uncontaminated. I'd hand the money to him anywhere he cared to name, but not here. Or I'd hand it to anyone who I was sure he'd sent. He said he'd ring me the next morning and tell me the final arrangements. There wasn't much time left, he said, before that freighter sailed and Brown was getting impatient."

"And that was on the Wednesday."

"Yes, the Wednesday. The next morning he gave me the instructions."

"I think we know the rest," I said. "You had to be on the Piccadilly up-platform at South Kensington at a certain time that Thursday afternoon. Someone would quickly convince you who he was and relieve you of the suitcase. Do you know who actually did take it?"

"I don't," she said. "I was trying to board the train in that dreadful crush and suddenly someone said, 'I'm Brown, Lionel's pal,' and the suitcase was taken before I hardly knew it. I'd been told not to look back. I don't think I could have, if I'd tried."

"And the voice? It belonged to the man who'd frightened you? The man who'd called himself Brown?"

"I don't know," she said. "It happened so suddenly. It was all so unreal. I thought afterwards it wasn't the same voice. It might have been Lionel's. He could have imitated the other voice. It wasn't like a speech. It was only three or four words."

"And you haven't been called by anyone since?"

"No one at all."

"And of course you haven't the faintest idea where your son might be? If he's not on a freighter bound for Canada?"

"I've no idea. I couldn't have. I do know that whenever I was rung, I had the impression he was talking from London."

That was all. Morchard glanced at us as if to ask if there were any more questions, then got to his feet. We rose, too. I told Lydia Morchard we were deeply grateful. We understood and respected the reasons that had actuated her and we hoped that everything would prove after all to have been for the best.

"Do sit down," Morchard said. "I'll see you again before you go. My wife's had a trying day. I think she should rest."

She gave us a little bow and a wan smile as he took her arm.

Hallows said he'd never thought he'd end up with a definite respect for Lydia Morchard. She'd had the hell of a time. That threat to harm the grandchildren must have been terrifying.

He was right, of course. She'd been gullible; incredibly gullible; on the other hand she'd had to work alone.

"I know it isn't very relevant," he said, "but I'd have liked to clear that poisoning business up."

I said she must have wanted Lionel to be careful. She told him she'd seen me with Morchard. Something like that. He took his own steps—amateurish ones—to see I didn't interfere.

Morchard came back. That elderly maid was following him with a tray.

"I'm sure you'd like tea before you leave," he told us. "It's been a trying day for you too."

When the room was clear and he'd poured the tea, he wanted our views on what we'd heard. He wished us to be frank.

"Then, frankly, we're agreed that your wife told us the truth. And the whole truth."

"That's a relief," he said. "The really promising thing seems to me to be that we've got rid of Lionel, at least for a time. What I'm really worried about now is that friend of his, or accomplice. A man like that could make a great deal of trouble."

"I don't think Brown ever existed," Hallows said.

Morchard stared.

"I think it was a purely solo swindle carried out by your stepson. All he had to do was find some shady acquaintance and school him carefully. When the so-called Brown spoke to your wife, he could have been reading his lines from a script. The whole thing wouldn't have cost more than a fiver."

"It was all an elaborate fraud?"

"Undoubtedly," I said. "Can you picture your stepson in the role of an organiser of that terrifically clever train robbery? Besides, we as good as know that he didn't arrive over here till about three months ago. Maybe much less. We could work out the times and let you know."

"And he may still be here now?"

"We think not. He's only too aware that the police are after him. If he has any sense he's somewhere abroad. My guess is France. He speaks the language. It shouldn't be too hard to make a new identity.

"One thing we feel we ought to make clear," I went on. "I take it you understand all the implications of what your wife has done. Disregarding, of course, her motives. What she's done is pay Danegeld. Nothing more or less.

When that money's gone, he'll be after more. Some new, plausible scheme. Or deliberate blackmail."

"I know," he said. "It's a frightening thought. It's a sword of Damocles. All she's done is buy a little time. Also there's that other frightening thing. The police may catch up with him."

"It has to be faced," I said. "I think our advice to you would be this: Be grateful for the respite and don't anticipate what may never happen." I smiled. "You remember your Virgil?"

"Yes," he said. "I think I do. I occasionally read him even now. Why'd you ask?"

"*Forsan et haec olim meminisse juvabit.* That's what I mean. One day it may even be a joy to look back on what's just happened."

"Maybe you're right," he said. "I hope so. With my wife, of course, it may not be so easy. She has far more at stake."

When we rose to go, I said that in our judgment the case was now over. There was nothing in the immediate future that we could possibly do. If, of course, we should glean anything from the police, we'd let him know at once. The only other thing was that question he'd raised about recouping our client for the racehorse swindle, and the loan company.

He said he'd like us to do that, provided always it could be done strictly anonymously. I said he could rely on us. And if at some future time trouble should again arise and he saw fit to employ us, we'd be happy to do all we could.

He shook hands warmly before he showed us out. "I'm more than grateful. And for the very tactful way you treated my wife. It was most considerate."

I hadn't regarded him as an emotional man, but there'd been emotion in his voice. When I looked back at the entrance gate he'd gone.

"A fine man," Hallows said.

I left it at that. As we made for the car I had a feeling of foreboding. That case was a long way from over. It would be quite a time before Henry Morchard became again the self he had been before that morning when he'd heard his wife at the telephone.

Two days later we sent in our account. A cheque, with renewed thanks, came by return of post. There was no trouble about paying off the loan company. They'd keep quiet for their own sakes. Isabel Herne was literally staggered to receive her own cheque, and she reminded me that I hadn't deducted the stipulated ten per cent. I insisted that I'd been joking. All I'd do was retain the twenty-five pounds we'd kept for eventualities.

We sent Henry Morchard a supplementary account, and again his cheque came back by return. One person whom I avoided was Sylvia Fairfield: in fact I never saw either of the Fairfields again. Why I didn't tell her, even in outline, what had happened was because I guessed that Morchard would see her himself. He'd probably want to know the truth about that suitcase. And he wouldn't want her any further implicated.

Christmas went by and the year ended. Occasionally I thought about the case. It had made too great an impression on me to be wholly forgotten. And there was the occasion in January when I happened to run across Matthews.

"Hallo, sir," he said, with a touch of the old heartiness. "Haven't seen you for quite a time. When was it?"

"At the Harringdon Hotel. Or was it later?"

"Funny about that crook," he said. "He must have taken that train at Victoria that night. And he's gone out of business. No one's heard a word of him since."

"Not even Interpol?"

"Not even Interpol. He's just disappeared into thin air."

"Lying doggo," I said. "He did have the best part of four thousand pounds to help out the loneliness, you know."

"That won't last for ever," he told me. "That's what we're betting on. Sooner or later he'll have to replenish the old coffers. You can't be lucky for ever."

"If you do ever catch up with him, you might let me know." He looked surprised. "I thought you'd finished with him."

"Officially, yes. Weeks ago. Just curious, that's all. And the satisfaction of knowing justice triumphant."

"Justice, my backside!" he said. "Curiosity, yes."

We were nearing the Greyhound in Prior Street and I said I'd stand him a drink. He said he was too busy. Some other time, maybe.

So much for that reminder of Lionel Palling. And so to the end of February. I was lunching at the club and, as usual, I'd got off the bus at Piccadilly Circus and was making the walk a kind of constitutional. Just before I reached the club, a taxi drew up, and who should get out of it but Henry Morchard. As soon as he'd paid off the driver, I joined him. He looked delighted to see me.

"You're staying to lunch?"

"No," he said. "I have an appointment at one. Thought I'd look in with the hope of running across an old friend or two."

"You'll let me stand you a drink?"

It was early and the bar was almost empty. He had a gin and tonic and I a beer. We took them to a corner seat. "And how are you?" I said.

"Fine," he said. "Couldn't be better."

"And your wife?"

"Pretty good. Between ourselves, she's never quite realised the full implications of what she did. Also she's up to the eyes electioneering. The word apparently got around that the General Election's coming soon."

"And yourself," I said. "You still find yourself looking up at that sword of Damocles?"

"Very rarely. Very rarely indeed."

I told him about that meeting with Matthews. Maybe there'd been some truth in that talk of going to Canada. If so, it would have been French-speaking Canada.

It was then that I thought of something: something that had suddenly emerged from a long way back.

"Tell me something," I said. "Strictly between ourselves. Were you really serious when you once told me that if you laid hands on your stepson you'd have your own solution?" He frowned. "What did I actually say?"

"That you'd strangle him with those two hands."

He grunted. "If I said it, I meant it. I was under great stress at the time. If I'd been faced with the choice of scandal and God knows what and letting him go on ruining other people's lives, I might have done just that. And I'd have done it in such a way that no one would ever have known." He gave a wry smile. "In my way, you know, I'm quite an efficient planner."

A shadow fell across the table. It was old Geoffrey Crewse of Crewse and Holt, the advertising people. He'd spotted Morchard too. I left them to it: said there was a man I was expecting to see if I could find him. When

I peeped in the bar just before lunch, Henry Morchard had gone.

March came in. It had been a grand winter compared with the one we'd suffered the previous year. Not that you notice too much the passing of the seasons when you live in a London flat and your life hovers somehow between it and Broad Street. I do know that some of Bernice's later hyacinths were still in bloom. I never tell her so but I hate the things. There's about them a scent of morgues and mortality.

About the middle of the month Jewle rang me about something or other, and I asked him if there'd been any developments in what we'd known as the Edward Gower case. He said as far as the Yard was concerned, the whole thing was in the files. It was the same with Interpol.

"Never knew anyone disappear so completely," he said. "You'd think he was dead. It's against all logic."

"How?"

"Figure it out," he said. "Put yourself in his place. He goes abroad. Anywhere you like. All he has is about four thousand pounds. And what's the first thing a chap like him would do? Buy a smart sports car. And make the round of the casinos. So how long would his money last?"

"Not long."

"Exactly. And yet he hasn't been trying any of his tricks again. It beats me."

"I wouldn't let it worry me," I told him. "Know what I think? The Salvation Army's got hold of him."

He laughed. A minute or two later I didn't feel like laughing. I'd happened to see a relationship between a couple of things. What Jewle had said had touched it off— *You'd think he was dead.* And Morchard had said he'd been prepared, given certain circumstances, to kill him.

Was that the truth? I didn't know. He was a man of whom I knew very little, but even a man you think you know well may startle you by his reactions to a crisis. If Morchard had seen yet more trouble for his wife, the Fairfields and himself, mightn't he have thought the only remedy was the removal of the cause?

But how? How could he have succeeded in laying hands on Palling when we had failed? And then I had a possible answer. He had known that his wife had discovered my identity. In his view, therefore, my chance of success was at once infinitely less. So what might he have done?

He was a wealthy man. He could have hired another firm of private detectives to act independently of ourselves. They had been on that South Kensington platform. They'd followed Palling with the suitcase to wherever it was that he'd been holed up. That had been the end of their assignment. Morchard had taken over.

In the next day or two my mind swayed this way and that. At one moment I couldn't believe that the Morchard whom I'd known that final day at The Cedars could have been driven to commit murder. But would he have regarded it as murder?

The mind can summon a queer logic and mightn't he have regarded it as a justifiable execution? In any case I wanted no truck or dealings with it and it was on that basis of determination that I at last managed to push it far back to the recesses of my mind.

Something, far later, was to bring it back. It was something to do with black magic. I'm serious. It was really black magic and it began on a Sunday evening towards the end of that same March.

PART III

11
A MATTER OF MAGIC

DAVE Jewle rang me that Sunday morning to say he might drop in on us some time in the evening. His children are married, and his wife, who used to be a hospital nurse, now helps at the local hospital, so he's sometimes at a loose end. Bernice likes Jewle. She took over the telephone and said he was to come early and have a meal with us.

Jewle duly turned up. While we were all having a short drink he asked if we were busy at the agency: too busy for me to take a morning off.

"If it's tomorrow morning I can manage it," I said. Bernice said of course I could manage it I spent far too much time at Broad Street.

"Wait a minute," I said. "What *is* this holiday? A job of work under another name?"

Jewle laughed. Nine men out of ten, he told Bernice, would have jumped at a nice little trip in the country.

"As a matter of fact," he said, "it's something to do with this black magic that's been cropping up in East Anglia. Did you see that programme on B.B.C. television a few weeks ago?"

We'd both seen it. And we'd both been highly sceptical. To call what had happened by the convenient name of black magic had seemed remarkably rash.

If we'd been in need of a topic of conversation, we definitely had one. The talk lasted all through the meal. But to get back to the proposed morning off. There'd been a certain happening some months previously at a ruined church in the Essex marshes. An old friend of Jewle—an Inspector Sparling had got into touch with him then but Jewle hadn't been able to make the trip. What he'd said was that if anything of the sort occurred again, then he'd like to be told. And something had happened. It had been discovered purely by chance on the Saturday morning and Sparling had rung as agreed.

"It's just that I'm sort of academically interested," Jewle told us. "It's not a criminal matter. Not like that pulling up of tombstones and writing on the church doors that happened in Sussex and elsewhere. That's been connected with black magic too but I'm a bit sceptical. What's happened at this Fenmarsh place looks more like the real thing."

That television programme had been about happenings in the lonely fen country of Norfolk. A long time ago villages were slowly wiped out through the ravages of malaria and the abandoned churches began their decay. Now they were little more than shells. Through drainage, the land had been largely redeemed but far too late to save the churches. And it was in them that the strange happenings had occurred.

"It's the same kind of thing at Fenmarsh," Jewle said, "except that that particular hamlet, so Sparling tells me, wasn't abandoned through sickness but because of inundations. There's the same little female figure with a thorn through the breast, and a black candle, and a black circle on the floor with a sheep's heart all over with thorns. According to Sparling, it's the most elementary type of black magic. He's keeping everything intact till we get there."

"You don't think it's some kind of hoax?" Bernice said. "Like ringing up an airport and saying there's a bomb in a plane?"

Jewle said he didn't know. He was keeping an open mind. I said my own idea was that it might have been done by gypsies. They were the likely surviving custodians of all sorts of forgotten mysteries.

"Could be," Jewle said. "As far as the Norfolk happenings are concerned, I don't think so. I admit this one may be a hoax but they were far too elaborate. There was a definite pattern. There was a specialist there, if you remember, explaining the whole thing. He took it seriously enough."

That was roughly how we left it. When Jewle went, it had been arranged that he'd pick me up at half-past nine the next morning.

It was a lovely morning of early spring. There was the luxury of a comfortable car with Jewle as driver. All I had to do was loll back or look around. Once we were through the outer suburbs we were in flat country interspersed with suburbanised villages; then these grew more sparse as we neared the sea. Fenmarsh was only a fifty-mile run. Jewle's rendezvous with Sparling was for eleven o'clock and, as we left a lonely country road and turned off into what was little more than a track, he said we'd comfortably make it.

It was lonely, marshy country with here and there an isolated farm and a few sheep grazing on the rare uplands. The road had once been metalled but now it was over-grown with grass and weeds. As we came in sight of the church, it petered out into a barely visible track with never a rut. It must have been many years since that track had been used.

Sparling was waiting for us just short of the church. He was a man of Jewle's age, competent-looking and quick in his movements. The church itself was an utter ruin. The roof had altogether gone as had parts of the walls. Except for gaps around its top, the tower was still standing. Every bit of timber had long since gone, and the floor was covered accumulated debris, with only here and there an open space. We threaded a way through the debris to one such space.

On the floor was a black circle of sprinkled soot about a yard in diameter. In the middle of it was the sheep's heart pierced with a score or more of thorns. To the left in a widish crack in the wall was a small, crudely fashioned female figure, a long thorn through its breast. Above it, on a slightly projecting ledge, was a black candle. It was about four inches tall and it looked as if it had been blown out before it had had a chance to gutter.

"What's it all about?" Jewle said.

Sparling said it was simple. It was a spell that had been cast in a case of jealousy, and almost certainly by a woman. Her man had been lured away by another woman.

"Like the mediaeval trick of sticking pins in a wax figure?"

"Exactly. A spell was cast on the woman and she'd either die or the man would leave her. I've looked it all up. It's a practice as old as history."

"All the same," Jewle said, "it doesn't explain this sudden recrudescence. Why has it begun popping up again?"

"Books," Sparling said. "Books on it are only recent, so interested parties have only just begun to take a hand in it."

"And this other rigmarole? This circle and the sheep's heart?"

"Accessories. Necessary accessories. All part of the spell. Sort of reinforcing it."

There wasn't much else to see. The weather had been uncommonly dry and there were no discernible footprints.

"That first case you had here some weeks ago," Jewle said. "Was it the same?"

"Much the same. Just a variation. Two of these figures. One without the thorn would be the one casting the spell and the other was the other woman. Otherwise the same."

"And the whole thing was publicised," Jewle said. "I saw it in my own paper, and some photographs. So couldn't this second affair be the work of some joker who'd seen an account of the first?"

Sparling shrugged his shoulders. It could be. But that didn't account for that first spell.

"Well, someone had to get here," Jewle said. "And it was a full moon. There wasn't much to carry, so whoever was responsible came on foot. A car might have been seen. Doesn't that rather suggest a purely local job?"

"It could be," Sparling said. "I haven't seen any new tyre marks. Mind you, the whole place was cut up a bit four months ago when the papers got hold of the story. Nowadays it's as quiet as it's ever been. Peters—he's the one who has the farm about a mile back—never sees a soul."

A dry hummock of debris lay against the wall in the sun. Jewle took out his pipe and spread his raincoat for a seat. Sparling was a pipe smoker too.

"Could you call all this consecrated ground?" Jewle said. "It was so once, of course."

I heard Sparling say something about lapse of ecclesiastical rights and then I was out of ear-shot. The small graveyard of that little church had once been enclosed by a low wall. You could trace the line of it, and here and there the last remnants of it still showed above the ground. In high summer the weeds must have been breast high. Now wind and weather had battered them down to a thick mat through which could be seen what was left of a tombstone. It was those remnants of tombstones that had caught my eye. Everything else, even that abomination inside the walls, was impersonal: they alone were the last personal remnants.

I walked around slowly over the soft mat of dead grass and weeds but it was time lost. Some there be, we are told, that have no memorial, and, as far as concerned the rude forefathers of this vanished hamlet, even their names had long since gone. Weather had flaked and eroded: even a stone that still looked sound was so smothered in lichen that, even when I used my pen-knife, its removal revealed only an occasional depression that might once have been a letter.

It was a pity. It might have been interesting to have read what had been carved on one of those ancient stones. I wondered if records had ever been taken while some were still decipherable and, as I made my way back towards the remnant of wall, I was thinking that Sparling might know. And then suddenly I was looking down at my feet.

Some of that thick mat of dead grass and weeds had been loose and my feet had moved it aside. A moment and I was moving the rest of it aside. Another moment and I was making for Jewle and Sparling. They were still arguing in the sun. I don't think they'd even missed me.

"How long since there was a burial here?"

Sparling looked surprised. "I don't know. Two hundred, three hundred years?"

"Then there's something you ought to see," I said. "I've just uncovered what looks like a fairly recent grave."

It did look like a grave. The mound was only a few inches high and about five feet long and two wide. The soil itself had been beaten down hard by the weather but you could see it had been roughly dug, with fragments of still-green weed and grass protruding everywhere among the dark earth.

"What d'you think?" Jewle said. "Is it some ritual burial connected with that mumbo-jumbo inside?"

"Might be," Sparling said. "But you're a gardener, like me. That soil was turned up before the frost got to it. We didn't get any hard frosts till mid-December."

"Then it might have been connected with that first happening late last October?"

"It could. In fact, it *has* to be. That soil hasn't been moved for months. If it is what you called a ritual burial, then it's something new. I've been reading up on it and no one's ever mentioned anything like it. Have you run across anything?"

"No," Jewle said. "All I've read is Harris's *Practice of Witchcraft* and nothing's said about it there." He turned to me. "You got any ideas?"

"None," I said. "Except perhaps one. This isn't consecrated ground, so why don't we find out what's there?"

"He's right," Jewle said. "Where can we get hold of a spade?"

Sparling knew. He and I set off in his car. Jewle stayed behind. We were making for the farm we'd seen in the near distance about a mile back. The house itself was wholly concealed by its buildings. As I told Sparling, a car could have made its way across the marshes to the church and nobody been aware. He said he hadn't thought of that. It could even have had its lights on. Not that it would have needed them. On Friday there'd been a full moon.

We branched off to a much better track and parked the car by a Dutch barn. There was a sound from somewhere inside. An elderly man was loading hay trusses on a trailer. Sparling called to him.

"Morning, Jim. Is the boss in?"

"No," he said. "Him and the missus have gone to Colchester."

"Then do you think you could find me a spade? And a trowel?"

"Reckon I might" He grinned. "What's happened then? You found some treasure or something?"

We set off back with the spade and trowel. Jewle was still standing by the grave. It was he who got to work first. The soil was moved to the side till one end was levelled and then he stuck the spade in. Even with the full weight of his foot it hadn't gone right down.

"Something here," he said.

"It couldn't be a stone?"

"Don't know," he said. "Better go a bit carefully all the same."

He worked with almost a flat spade, scooping the soil towards the edges. He'd cleared about six inches when he drew back.

"There's something here. I can smell it."

"So can I," Sparling said. "Even over here."

Think I'll work with the trowel," Jewle said. "You start clearing the other end."

He got his pipe going full blast, spread his raincoat for a kneeling-pad and set to work. Sparling got busy with the spade. I drew a little way back. I'd had that musty smell in my nostrils too, and I didn't like to think what might be in that shallow grave. Jewle and Sparling are hardened cases. Curious I may be, but there's something so grimly final about a corpse that the sight of one always makes me uneasy.

So I stood there watching. A gull moved suddenly over-head as if it was curious too, then Jewle called Sparling over and the two got busy at Jewle's end. A couple of minutes and they got to their feet. Jewle beckoned to me.

No more than six inches below the original surface was a deeper, cleared space: a rough circle of a foot or so in diameter. In it was framed a skull: the skull of someone old. A fringe of white hair still lay about its top.

"Recent?" I said. "Or old?"

"Last October probably," Jewle said. "Maybe we'd better talk this over. After all, we've got all day."

Jewle and Sparling were going on with their uncovering. I was sent off to the market town to get into touch with Sparling's Chief Constable. I was also to ring the Yard and say Jewle mightn't be back till late. His stomach was far stronger than mine. I'd also to bring back some sandwiches and a couple of bottles of beer.

It was past one o'clock when I got back. The Chief Constable, I said, would be along in the course of the next half-hour.

"Have a look now," Jewle said. "There's no particular smell."

The skeleton lay on its side, knees slightly drawn up.

"A lot of acid probably in this soil," Jewle said. "Decomposition must have set in quickly."

I nodded. For a moment I didn't feel like talking.

"Probably a woman," he said. "An old woman, as you see."

"Yes," I said. "And what now?"

"We've been talking it over," he said. "Sorry to have spoiled your day but we think you should go back, leave the car at the station and take either a bus or a train. I'm likely to be here for hours."

I did as I was told. The station sergeant told me there'd be a train at two-fifteen. I didn't feel much like eating but I had a late lunch at a hotel to pass the time. The train was a slow one and I didn't get back to Broad Street till half-past three. I stayed there till six in case Jewle should ring. He didn't, and I went home.

It was after seven o'clock when he did ring me. He was all apologies for having, as he said, messed up my day. I asked him where he was speaking from and he said his office.

"There was a lot to do," he said. "Measurements, photographs and all that. Then I had to persuade the local people we could handle things better here. I had to wait till our own people got there to take soil samples and so on. Also it was a pretty tricky job removing that skeleton intact. The forensic people are busy on it right now."

"You're going to publicise it?"

"Of course," he said. "Soon as there's anything to publicise. I doubt if that'll be before tomorrow."

For Bernice, the flat and Broad Street are worlds apart. She never asks questions. But since the whole thing would almost certainly be in the next day's evening papers, I told her about my day. She was incredibly shocked. She wanted to know if it really was a ritual burial.

"Jewle and Sparling didn't know," I said. "All they had was ideas. If the woman was buried there at the time of that first black magic business last October, there might be a connection. Then there were two female figures: one pierced with a thorn and one not. The old woman couldn't very well have been the one who'd enticed someone's husband away, so she might have been the other one. If so, that business last October may have been a kind of announcement that the matter had been concluded. Concluded because the aggrieved party was dead. This last mumbo-jumbo was an announcement that the guilty party was now dead, too."

"You actually believe all that?"

"I don't," I said. "Not because it mayn't be true but because I just know nothing about it. I doubt if the Psychic Research experts do either. Not that that'll stop them giving their views in the press."

It was not till around eleven o'clock the next morning that Jewle rang me.

"Well," he said, "we know practically everything now. The body was deposited about four months ago. Soil acidity and humidity apparently prove it. Also they ran a carbon test. The woman was probably in the early seventies, about five-foot eight. Slight curvature of the spine: a sort of stoop you get in old age. She'd probably been in indifferent health before she died. A natural death, by the way. The head of the right femur was fractured. A broken hip, if you like, and it hadn't been pinned. What probably happened was that she broke it and then bronchial pneumonia set in. I'm told that's the run of events in very many similar cases."

"You're giving it full publicity?"

"The fullest," he said. "We'd like her doctor to come forward, but that's a longer shot than you'd think. For one thing there're no end of such cases and also a doctor mayn't have been consulted. Wasn't something said about gypsies being mixed up in all this hoodoo? If she was a gypsy, I doubt if there'd have been a doctor."

The mid-afternoon editions carried the story. Banner head-lines shrieked across the pages. One enterprising paper had managed to get an expert opinion. In half a column he'd managed to say nothing that we hadn't heard or surmised already. The rest of the experts would be in full spate in the morning.

They were. My own two papers aren't of the shrieking type, but the story had plenty of prominence. Those happenings in Norfolk and Sussex were recalled and comparisons made. There were slabs of history and parallels. One expert even cited a similar happening among the Shoshones of Wyoming. The whole thing still left me an unbeliever. And Jewle too. When he rang me later that afternoon, he put the whole thing in a sentence.

"Far as I'm concerned, I've got a skeleton."

His job was to identify the woman and investigate an unlawful burial: not a burial in what had once been consecrated ground but a secret burial in no matter what ground. That the woman had died a natural death had also nothing to do with it. If someone mentioned gypsies and the Big Bugs insisted, then he'd enquire among gypsies. He didn't want to know why but who. Who had buried an old woman in that lonely grave.

*

A day or two went by and the story was relegated to the back pages. Jewle rang again. He asked if I'd seen his appeal to doctors. It had had to be specially worded—a doctor who had attended an elderly woman with a fracture of the femur and who had probably died without—and there was the point—without his having been aware of a funeral. The time—late October or early November.

There'd been no results. Another day or two and the case had disappeared altogether from the press. Other things—according to your taste in newspapers—had taken its place. Things were still pretty grim in Cyprus and Vietnam. More trouble looked likely over Berlin. There was speculation over the Budget and, more earth-shaking, a film star had left her husband for a pop-singer: "LOVE COMES FIRST, SAYS MAYBELLE."

Even Jewle was thinking of relegating the whole thing to the files. I had lunch with him about a fortnight after that dramatic Saturday and we talked the whole thing over again. It was something that I, certainly, would never be likely to forget.

But I did forget it. By the time April was well on the way I was remembering it at only rare moments. I'd have remembered it at rarer moments still if something hadn't happened. Mind you, it had nothing to do with that strange burial. What it did recall was the Edward Gower/Lionel Palling affair, and it was due to a call from Isabel Herne.

12

BACK TRAIL

IT WAS in the middle of the morning that Isabel rang me. She said she'd rung Bernice to suggest lunch but Bernice had apparently been out.

"She said something about going out," I said, "but I'm afraid I can't contact her. I'm sure she'd have been delighted. You're in town for the day?"

She said she had an appointment that afternoon with her solicitors. "But what about you?" she said. "Are you free for lunch?"

I regretted I wasn't.

"Then what about a drink? At about twelve."

I didn't see why not. Half-an-hour with Isabel would be a pleasant change. An hour and a half over lunch might have been something of a trial. We agreed on the Café Royal at twelve.

We had quite a chat. She'd completely recovered, she told me frankly, from that dreadful business at Cambridge. In a way it had done her an awful lot of good.

She might have been leading up to the question of the recovery of her money: at any rate that was the question she asked next. I said the matter was a strictly confidential one: something between the police and the agency.

"But about yourself," I went quickly on. "You haven't bought that top-class hunter you were looking for?"

She hadn't—as yet. What she was thinking of doing was to commission a trainer to buy one at the Dublin sales.

"I hope you'll be lucky," I told her. "If you are, then you'll be very lucky indeed."

She didn't see it, so I explained. There'd be the horse's winnings. Also the only safe horse to bet on was your own, and what you made wasn't subject to tax.

She laughed. "You should buy a horse yourself. But seriously, I don't like betting. Just a bit for fun if I'm on a course. I'm not a puritan but I honestly think there's far too much betting. Since the Act came in, do you know how many betting shops there are? Over twenty thousand! I know because I saw a programme on it on television."

That's a short extract from half-an-hour's talk, or chatter. Now there's something I'd like to explain. I may have said it many times before but it has to be said again.

I'm the sort of person who hates loose ends and unsolved problems. They tease at me and nag like a bad tooth. Even an unsolved clue in a crossword can keep me awake at night. Maybe it's all due to a disproportionate sense of my own capabilities, but there it is. It isn't that I hate to be beaten. I just want to know.

As I sat in my office that afternoon, whatever kind of computer it is that I happen to have in my brain began presenting me with something that had long since been stored. Over twenty thousand betting shops. That'd be in England and Wales. And what would be the share of London? Say a sixth or a fifth. Best part of four thousand betting shops in Greater London alone.

Another minute and I was reaching for pad and pencil. I'd given Hewes a tip about betting shops and he'd acted on it. He'd rung shop after shop till he'd found the one frequented by our man. How long would it take per shop?

I took off my watch and laid it beside the pad. I rang an imaginary shop. I asked to speak to the manager. I explained what I wanted. I gave a description of the man. He told me to hang on while he looked in the shop. He came back and said he thought the man I was interested in was there. I thanked him and gave assurances that there'd be no trouble, then he rang off. And the time taken was just over four minutes. But I'd made everything go like clockwork. Taking an average, five minutes would be the better time.

Twelve calls an hour, working non-stop. Ninety-six for an eight-hour shift, going full blast. And Hewes had been at the job no more than three days at the most. So at the most he couldn't have tried more than three hundred shops. He hadn't even scratched the surface! And yet the last of those three hundred had been the very one. What was it then? Colossal luck? Or had there been something fishy?

I thought for a minute or two, then rang the loan company. Hackle was in. He was most genial. The magic return of five hundred pounds plus had been a magnificent lubricant.

"Just a friendly call," I said. "How are you?"

"Fine," he said. "It's the good winter we've had. And you?"

"Keeping pretty fit. And our mutual friend Hewes?"

"He's gone." he said. "I thought I told you about it."

"So you did," I said. "Where's he gone? Somewhere in the country?"

"To tell the truth I haven't heard from him. When I last saw him, he hadn't made up his mind."

"He sold the business?"

"Yes. To Decklow Enquiries. They're working with us now."

"I'd thought Peplow might have been able to buy it."

"No." he said. "Even if he'd been able to raise the money I don't think he'd have liked the responsibility."

"You happen to know where he is?"

He asked me to wait. He had it somewhere. "Ah! here it is."

He gave me the details and I could hardly believe my luck. Peplow had been taken on by Tom Jordan! His is one of the two agencies with whom we have a working agreement. If they're short of an operative, we try to lend one and, if we're short, we can call on them.

I rang off and did some more thinking. A minute or two and I was ringing Tom. An amiable word or two and I came to the point.

"Haven't you taken on a man named Peplow?"

"That's right," he said. "A good man. I've known him for years. Used to work for a little agency run by a man called Hewes."

"That's the man," I said. "I just want a word with him about something that happened while he was working with Hewes. Do you know where I can find him?"

"I think so. You know the Claverhouse Hotel just off Dover Street? You'll find him somewhere round there."

I took the Underground and got off at what used to be Dover Street station. The Claverhouse was about five minutes away. Tom Jordan handles divorce cases, so Peplow might be propped up against a nearby wall behind a newspaper. He wasn't. I looked around and there was no sign of him. Then he all at once appeared as from nowhere. He'd been parked in a tea-shop just across from the hotel.

"Thought I recognised you," he said. "Didn't know you were looking for me."

"Shan't keep you a minute," I said. "It's something to do with that old Gower case. The one who gave us the slip at the Harringdon. The case has popped up again and I'm working on it. So tell me something. Where exactly was that betting shop where you saw him?"

"I thought you knew. One in Quincy Street. About five minutes from the hotel."

"And you actually saw him there?"

"Yes, sir: I did. And when he came out I followed him to the Harringdon."

"That's right. I remember now." I held out my hand. "Sorry you couldn't help. By the way, how's Hewes?"

"Don't know," he said. "Can't make it out, not unless something's happened to him. We used to be pretty close. It's over four months now."

"He never gave you an idea of where he'd be going when he retired?"

"Well, I think he fancied Cornwall. Somewhere by the sea."

"Somewhere good for his bronchial tubes."

"That's right," he said. "One day he'd be all right and then he'd have a day or two when he'd hardly get his breath."

"Well remember me to him when you do hear from him."

I waved a hand as I moved off. Not that I was particularly cheerful. The hard facts were that Lionel Palling had been in that betting shop and that Peplow had followed him to the Harringdon Hotel. I'd been wrong. I'd discounted the element of chance. Hewes hadn't rung more than three hundred betting shops but the last one he'd rung had been the one in Quincy Street.

When Bertha brought in coffee the next morning, some trick of the mind made me hark back to Quincy Street and what Peplow had told me. If I wanted to spread myself I'd say I was a sifter for the truth. One of those truths is that I'm of a most suspicious nature. Something, somewhere, had been telling me that everything had not been all it had seemed. Perhaps I was peeved that those stop-watch calculations of mine had proved nothing and that Hewes had had a lot of luck. I don't know. All I do know is that I suddenly knew it might be worth my time to drop in on the manager at Quincy Street.

I found it with no great trouble. Racing wouldn't be on for well over two hours, but a couple of prospective clients were looking up form. Elderly men: glad of something to pass their time. Beyond one of the receipt and pay grilles a man was working. I asked him if I could see the manager. He wanted my name, so I gave him an agency card. A couple of minutes later I was being shown into an office. The manager—name of Hartwright—was younger than I'd thought. He was courteous enough but his eyes had a mighty hard look. He was twiddling my card in his hand.

"You're the Mr. Travers?"

"Yes," I said. "I operate the detective agency. I'm making enquiries about one of your previous customers. He didn't actually swindle you but he was a crook. The police want him too."

He raised his eyebrows. He waved a hand. "Sit down, sir. One of my customers, you say?"

"That's right. You'll treat what I'm telling you as confidential?"

He waved his hand again. "Go ahead."

"Three people were after him," I said. "The police, myself, and another private detective employed by a loan company. The last one had the luck. He knew this character liked a gamble so he had the idea he might be using a betting shop. He began calling them and after three days he rang you. He described the man and you had a look and spotted him. A tail was stationed outside and the man was followed. Unfortunately he pulled a smart trick and got clear."

His eyes had been narrowing. He leaned across his desk. "What is this? Some sort of bad joke?"

"Good lord, no," I said. "I can tell you who the man was who saw him here and followed him. Better still, ring Scotland Yard and ask to speak to an Inspector Matthews. He handled it from the police side."

I sat back. His hand went towards the telephone. "I might do just that."

I made no comment. His hand came back. "What was this crook like?"

I described him. I said if he rang the Harringdon Hotel the manager would remember me, and that the man had been staying there as an Australian. He'd operated under quite a few aliases.

"No one rang me about such a man. And I don't remember him. Hundreds of people use this shop on a busy afternoon."

"No one rang you?"

"No one rang me. I've been here ever since we opened and never been absent a day, except for a holiday last February."

"Couldn't the detective have rung one of your people?"

"Never a hope. It's not their business. There's a special office through there to deal with calls. Anything like what you say would have been referred at once to me."

He smiled.

"I'll tell you something else. If I had received such a call, do you know what I'd have done? I'll tell you. Sweet Fanny Adams. A business like this depends on confidence between us and the client. And since we're talking in confidence, I'll tell you something else. Even if the police had rung, I'd have known nothing. I don't say that later on I wouldn't have handled it myself."

I got up. "Somebody's obviously made a fool of me. I'd still like you to have a word with Inspector Matthews. We're a reputable firm, Mr. Hartwright. We don't go round playing jokes on people."

"Forget it." He reached across the table and we shook hands. "I've been made a monkey of in my time. Just forget it."

It was about the last thing I could do. In a way it had been a startling revelation. Hewes had lied to me. Those calculations of mine had been right.

I don't remember actually boarding the bus that took me back to Broad Street. The more I thought, the less sense I saw. Palling *had* been in that betting shop. Peplow had actually seen him there. Later he'd followed him to the Harringdon. And it was Hewes who had known Palling was in that betting shop. He had given Peplow his orders. How then had Hewes discovered he'd be there?

The whole thing just didn't make sense. The police, with all their resources, had been on the hunt for the man they knew under various aliases. We'd been anxious to find him too, and yet Hewes—acting entirely on his own— had been the one to find him. No man, surely, could have had that kind of luck.

It was when I'd got off the bus and was walking to Broad Street that I thought I had the answer. Maybe Hewes in his time had come to know quite a few shady characters. Maybe he had caught up with Palling in quite another way. There'd been something about it that might have reflected discredit on himself and so he'd cooked up that yarn about getting into touch with the Quincy Street manager.

It had to be the answer. In any case, that was where I left it. Until the following morning. It was Bertha, bringing in coffee again, that set off some more thinking. The upshot was that I rang Hackle.

"This is Travers again, Mr. Hackle. Sorry to bother you once more but I've been thinking about Hewes. This may sound a funny question, but was he, to your knowledge, anything of a betting man?"

"Hewes!" He laughed. "Good God, no! That was about the last thing he'd do."

"Why do you say that? We all have our little secret vices—if you can call it a vice. So why not Hewes? Did you ever hear him say anything against it?"

"Can't say I did. But it wasn't his nature. He was a bit religious in his way."

It was like extracting some tricky teeth. I asked in what way.

"Well, he took an interest in religious matters. He was a sidesman at the local church. He always closed down on a Sunday. Can't say I ever knew him work on a Sunday. I don't say he didn't let Peplow carry on. But not Hewes. Not Norman Hewes."

"Sorry I bothered you. It was just an idea. You may or may not remember there was a betting shop tied up in that fiasco at the Harringdon Hotel. I just wondered if Hewes had had some private information. As a customer himself, if you know what I mean. He lived at Stratford, didn't he?"

"That's right. 121 Latchway Avenue. But he isn't there now, you know."

"I know," I said. "You told me. Forget the whole thing. And thanks again."

I should have been satisfied but I wasn't. I'd never been in Hewes's company more than a couple of hours at the most, and it was only natural that there should be things about him that I'd never suspected, and yet I was far from happy. Something kept telling me that I ought to know a whole lot more. Maybe it was a hunch, or a loose end. I couldn't have told you, but I knew what I wanted to do and I didn't care where I went to do it I wanted to know how it was that Hewes had made that rapid contact with Palling.

It was just after two o'clock when I stepped off a bus and looked about me. *"Now am I in Arden, the more fool I."* That had been Touchstone. For my own part, now was I in Stratford and I too was probably a fool.

Stratford, I said to myself. Stratford-atte-Bowe. In Chaucer's days it had been open fields. Somewhere there'd been a nunnery where a young novice had learned to speak French. Now it had miles of marshalling yards, canals, factories everywhere, bustling pavements and grim streets.

I set off in quest of Latchway Avenue. It turned out to be a street with semi-detached houses. Hewes's old house was at a road junction, and its beautifully-kept garden ran along Wicklow Road. At its end was an asbestos garage with a concrete run-in and small twin gates. I walked back to Latchway Avenue. Beyond its end was the spire of a church.

I made my way there. A notice board just inside the gate said it was St. Martha's and the vicar a Stanley

Allman. A passer-by pointed out the vicarage. I pushed the door-bell.

The Rev. Stanley Allman was a middle-aged man with a friendly face. When I said I was a friend of Hewes and was making enquiries about him, he asked me to come in. We went into his study.

"So you're a friend of my old friend Norman Hewes," he said. "You know he's left the district?"

"I learned it only a day or so ago," I said. "I'd rather like to get in touch with him but no one seems to know where he's gone. You've had news of him yourself?"

He shook his head.

"No. Why, I don't know. I thought he'd have written me. When he came to say goodbye he said he was buying a place in Cornwall." He shook his head again. "I can't help thinking that something may have happened to him. He didn't enjoy very good health, you know. The change mayn't have been good for him."

"I know," I said. "You think that was the only reason why he retired? That and his age, of course."

"An accumulation of worries," he said. "And when he lost his housekeeper he couldn't face the prospect of living alone. He'd seen it coming, of course. She was getting very frail."

"I never met her. My dealings with him were always in town."

"A nice old lady," he said. "A distant relation, I believe. She'd been with him for years."

I frowned. "Wait a minute. I believe he did mention her. What was her name, now?"

"Garland," he said. "Rachel Garland. She passed away some four or five months ago. Buried in East-gate Cemetery. Hewes asked me to officiate myself as a personal favour but I'd have been glad to anyway. She was a regular attendant here for years."

I held out my hand. I said I was most grateful. I gave him my name and the flat address. If Hewes should write. I'd be glad to have his news.

I walked slowly back to Latchway Avenue. My brain was churning away at impossible ideas. For a moment in that vicarage study I'd had one wild idea and then, in the next moment, I'd known how wild it really was. And yet everything had been curiously pat. If only there'd been no funeral. If only I'd asked a few more questions. But I *could* ask more questions. Maybe there *was* someone who could tell me a whole lot more that I wanted to know. No one knows so much about you as a neighbour.

I knocked at the door of Number 119. It was opened by a tall and rather stout woman who looked about sixty. There was no hostility in her enquiring look. I raised my hat.

"Sorry to trouble you but I've been looking for an old friend of mine, a Mr. Hewes. They've just told me at the vicarage that he's left the district. I wonder if you could tell me anything."

She asked me to come in. From the tiny hall we stepped into the living-room. I gave her an agency card.

"My name's Travers. May I ask your name?"

"Poole. Dora Poole."

"Thank you, Mrs. Poole. As you see, I run a detective agency just as Mr. Hewes did. We occasionally worked together. That's why I wanted to see him now. To tell the truth, I hoped he might be able to undertake some work for me."

She asked me to sit down.

"Mr. Hewes has gone," she said. "Must be four months by now. He was buying a little place in Cornwall."

"You have the address?"

"I haven't," she said, just a bit tartly. "After all I did you'd have thought he'd have let me know. Unless something's happened to him. You say you've seen Mr. Allman?"

"Yes," I said. "He hasn't heard either. He thinks like you. Mr. Hewes could be dead and buried and no one know a thing about it. If I remember rightly, he didn't have any relatives."

"Only Mrs. Garland. She was a sort of second cousin. Like him, in a way. I mean he was a widower and she was a widow. Lost her husband in the first war."

"You knew her pretty well?"

She smiled. "She was a regular old dear. I used to call her Rache. For Rachel. That was her name, see. We used to spend a lot of time together. Always in and out of each other's houses till she took ill."

"Must have been awkward with Mr. Hewes away."

"Wasn't awkward at all," she said. "My daughter's out all day so I used to pop in every now and again. Even when she had to take to her bed, I looked after her. Norman—that's Mr. Hewes—wanted to pay me but I wouldn't hear of it."

"That was very good of you. Was she ill very long?"

"About two months. You could see she wasn't going to get over it. She was over seventy, you know. What happened that afternoon was that she tried to get out of bed and she fell—poor old dear. I went in to make her a cup o' tea and there she was, laying on the floor."

"She was hurt?"

"Oh, yes. She was moaning about her side. The doctor found she'd broken her hip."

"You fetched the doctor?"

"Soon as I got her back in bed. Dr. Edwards. It's only in Wicklow Road."

"And you actually managed to get her back into bed yourself?"

She smiled. "It was like picking up a baby."

I shook my head admiringly.

"You were what the Bible calls a good neighbour. It's a pity there aren't more like you about. And I suppose it was the fall that really killed her."

"Well, that and her being so weak already. The doctor couldn't do nothing for her, only make her comfortable. That was the Friday and she died on the Tuesday. Pneumonia it was. I helped to lay the poor old dear out. The funeral was on the Saturday. That was the 6th. I remember because it was my Doris's birthday on the Sunday. There was only him and me and Doris at the funeral, and the vicar. She never really had no friends except us."

I got to my feet.

"I'm most grateful to you, Mrs. Poole. You have my name and address, so if Mr. Hewes does write to you, will you let me know?"

It was a longish walk back to the main shopping centre. It was almost four o'clock. I found a Lyons and had a cup of tea and a cake. What I wanted still more was to get off my feet and do some hard thinking.

Suppose, I said: suppose that, in spite of that funeral, the body of Rachel Garland had somehow been transported to that ruined church in the Essex marshes. Everything about the dead woman corresponded with what was known about the anonymous corpse. And added to it all was the apt retirement of Hewes and his total disappearance. How could that transportation possibly have been done. That Hewes had probably had a car had little to do with it. You just can't open a deep grave in a public cemetery, take out a corpse and replace the soil and leave no trace of the exhumation.

And even if Hewes had been able miraculously to do all that, then why? Surely a man so staid as he had seemed and so set in his suburban ways, couldn't have been a member of some secret, crack-pot cult? In any case there were grounds at least for various suppositions. Everything told me that I should at least ring Jewle. But how could I? I might find myself struggling in far too deep waters. I might even have to reveal the true identity of the man he'd known under all sorts of names that weren't his own. At all costs, I told myself, the Morchards and the Fairfields had to be protected against publicity. Except, perhaps, in the case of Lydia Morchard, it was something they'd neither caused nor deserved. And there remained the matter of the agency's own reputation and given word.

I fetched myself a second cup of tea and did some more thinking. In a minute or two I began to see a way. Maybe Jewle needn't ever have to know about Lionel Palling. It would mean wary walking but I'd done that kind of thing before. Another few moments and I was finishing off my tea. I asked the way to the main post office and it was from there that I rang Jewle.

13
MOST OF A MYSTERY

"That body you dug up at Fenmarsh," I said. "Anything happened about it?"

"Nothing. Nothing whatever. Why do you ask?"

"I may have stumbled on something. I think you ought to hear it."

"What sort of something?"

"I'll tell you when I see you. I think you ought to join me here straight away. I'm at Stratford."

"Stratford! You don't mean Stratford-on-Avon?"

"Stratford, London. You could be here in half-an-hour. I'll be waiting outside the main post office."

I rang off. He couldn't get in touch with me to do any more questioning, so he'd have to come. When he did come it was in an easily spotted police car and I waved him in at the space reserved for mail vans. It was the only parking space I'd been able to find. He was alone and I got in beside him.

"Glad you could come," I told him placatingly. "I think you're going to find it interesting."

He shook his head. Annoyance or amusement?

"You're the most extraordinary cove. You suddenly pop up out here in the wilds—" He broke off. "What's this you say you've found?"

"It goes back a bit. You remember our friend Edward Gower, etc., etc., who finally did a disappearing act at the Harringdon Hotel? In case you've forgotten any of the details, I'd like to tell you how we got on to him. Why we went to pick him up at the hotel."

I told him the whole story. It even included my calculations on the time taken to ring betting shops.

"Wait a minute," he said. "You told me you'd finished with that case."

"So I had. But that didn't stop me thinking about it. You know me. I just can't let things alone. I thought something was wrong and it'd go on nagging at me unless I had some sort of answer. Hewes himself wasn't available so I thought I'd make some enquiries in his native borough."

"Which is what you've been doing."

"Exactly. But about that body we unearthed. Your broadcast appeal mentioned a broken femur, but when you were able to see the whole skeleton clearly, did you notice anything about the ribs?"

"A couple were broken," he said. "Sparling thought he might have done it himself. Those bones were pretty fragile, you know."

That was all I needed. I suggested he get out his notebook : there might be things he'd like to take down. There were. By the time I'd finished, he'd covered a couple of pages.

"Incredible!" he said. "She's made to measure. It must have been her."

"Except for the little matter of a funeral."

"I know," he said. "You got the name of the under-takers?"

I told him I hadn't wanted to make Dora Poole suspicious. She'd talked and I'd encouraged her. What she thought now wouldn't matter. She'd tell him who the undertakers were.

"Even the dates fit," I said. "She died on December the 2nd and was buried on Saturday the 6th. If she ever was buried."

"She couldn't have been," he said. "There's only one explanation. Hewes substituted something that weighed about the same and then took her to Fenmarsh."

"But why? Surely he couldn't have been mixed up in that black magic stuff?"

"You never know," he said. "After all, just how much did you know about him?"

"Practically nothing. In fact I'd say that I've learned more about him the last day or two than I ever knew. But you can be in a much better position. You can talk to

Peplow. And the two Poole women. And the vicar. Hewes may have had some arguments about black magic with Allman. He spoke of him as a friend."

He looked at his watch. "The one I'd like to talk to is the doctor. You know where he lives?"

It was only a matter of finding a number. He backed the car out and we headed for Latchway Avenue. We turned into Wicklow Road and he slowed the car to a crawl. We saw the brass plate at another road junction about half-way along.

A pretty woman in the late thirties opened the surgery door. From somewhere inside the house came the laughter of children.

"Mrs. Edwards?"

"Yes," she said. "You want to see my husband? I'm afraid he's having his tea."

"We can wait," Jewle told her. "Will you tell him I'm a police officer? We think he can help us in some enquiries."

She looked a bit startled. Edwards must have been surprised too: it wasn't a minute before he joined us in that waiting-room. He looked about forty: a shortish man, squarely built and balding on top. There were introductions and handshakes and we all got seated.

"This is strictly confidential," Jewle said. "As a medical man, you'll realise the importance of that. You know about that case of an elderly woman whose body was dug up in the Essex marshes?"

"Indeed, yes. My wife also drew my attention to that appeal you made. To be perfectly frank, I thought at first I had a case something like it myself, but this particular patient was buried in the normal way."

"You're referring to a Rachel Garland?"

He stared. Jewle smiled. "Nothing to be alarmed about, doctor. Nothing will probably arise but, even if it does, I'll ensure that you're not in any way involved. I'm sure she received the best possible medical attention, so would you mind telling us about—well, the later phases."

He found the Rachel Garland case-history in his files. What Dora Poole had told me absolutely tallied.

"Yes," he said. "Mrs. Poole fetched me. I happened to be in and I had the car at the kerb so I went along at once." He gave a wry smile. "Mrs. Poole's a jewel of a woman but I did wish she'd left her where she'd found her. I knew, of course, there was nothing I could do. She had been and was a very sick woman. All I could do was keep her under sedation to ease the pain. No use getting her to a hospital, or binding the ribs or doing anything about the fracture of the femur. I was surprised she lasted as long as she did. There was no hesitation about signing the death certificate. The ultimate cause, of course, was bronchial pneumonia."

Jewle rose. I followed.

"That's more than satisfactory, Doctor." He gave a wry smile of his own. "You may think we're a bit pedantic, following up every possible case, but it has to be done."

Edwards smiled too. "I know. The wheels of God."

"Something like that," Jewle said, and held out his hand. "You've been most helpful, Doctor, and we do appreciate it. Sorry we had to snatch you away from your tea."

Edwards walked with us to the car. Jewle said nothing till we'd turned back into Latchway Avenue. I thought he was going to stop at 119 but he drove on. Just as we neared the end, he did pull the car up. He said he didn't like talking and driving.

"It was those damn ribs," he said. "But for that we might have been on to her days ago. That Edwards is a sensible man."

"And what now?"

"I'll look around," he said. "Ask a few questions. Not that I'm not sure of my own mind. It was that Rachel Garland who was buried at Fenmarsh. And it was your man Hewes who did it. Tell me: do you think there's any truth in what some people seem to think—that he might be dead?"

"Could be," I said. "All I know is that a very few days after his housekeeper died, he'd sold up, lock, stock and barrel, and gone. And no one's heard from him since: even those he ought to have written to."

"Cornwall, you said."

"That's what he'd always hinted at. He had occasional bronchial attacks and sea air might have been good for it."

He drove on. Traffic was bad and it got much worse. It was only at stops that we had a few words and what was said amounted to very little. We came to the Yard by way of the Embankment. I'd said I'd walk the short way to the flat.

He wasn't grudging in his thanks: all there was was a little something that told me he hadn't given enthusiastic credence to everything I'd said. My old nurse used to say that if I'd only gulp down the first dose of some obnoxious medicine, all subsequent ones would never be noticed. Not that I was crowing about Jewle's swallowing that initial dose. What might be more difficult would be to get him to swallow the second.

He gave me a courtesy call the following afternoon. He'd had a busy half-day at Stratford. He'd initiated enquiries in Cornwall, with Devon and Somerset thrown in for luck. It was a big area and he wasn't too hopeful of results. Still, there was plenty of time.

I didn't ring Jewle again till the Monday morning. There was something I'd like to talk over with him: something to do with the Norman Hewes case. He was busy, he said, so perhaps I could come along.

Jewle in his room and Jewle in our flat are very different people. He's never rude, but sometimes he's uncommonly direct.

"I can't make you out," he said. "Why're you going to all this bother? You say you're not working for a client, so what's really on your mind?" He gave a dry smile. "Unless you feel you've got to do your duty as citizen."

"Maybe it's that," I said. "But tell me something. Just how seriously are you taking this case?"

"Well, it's a tricky one to place. All the same, it's got to be cleared up. Hewes has to be questioned. What the charge'll be I frankly don't know. It'll be for the D.P.P. to decide. Between ourselves, it might be what I said—burial in an unlawful place. Something like that."

"And what if it isn't? What if it's—well a capital offence?"

"How could it be? The woman died a natural death."

"I know. But let me put something up to you. Suppose Hewes didn't fill that coffin with ballast. Suppose he removed one body and substituted another?"

He stared. "You're not serious?"

"I am. I may be all wrong but I think you ought to hear what I've got to say. Tell me this, for instance. Why should Hewes disappear? In the ordinary course of events he was retiring. He was going somewhere in the country and he'd be keeping in touch with his old friends. Wouldn't that be normal?"

"Carry on."

"Very well, then: I repeat the question. Why did he disappear? No one had the least idea that Mrs. Garland's burial wasn't a normal interment. No one could possibly be expected to find that body at Fenmarsh. Another month or two and that grave would have been overgrown with grass and weeds. But for an amazing stroke of bad luck— for Hewes—she'd have been undisturbed till Judgment Day. On the other hand, if another body was in the coffin, that'd be different. He'd be living under the threat of a murder charge, so he made a sort of clean break. He wanted the whole business out of his mind. That's why he's disappeared. Why even his closest friends haven't had a word from him."

"Very well," he said. "Assume all that. Now tell me whose the body is."

"Let's get right down to the roots," I told him. "You know about Hewes and why he was looking for the man I first knew as Edward Gower. I've told you there was something suspicious about the way Hewes ran Gower to earth at the Harringdon. There was something fishy about that whole episode and I'm pretty sure that Hewes had made contact before that. And he didn't turn him in because Gower made it well worth his while. Gower'd been lying low and he couldn't have spent much of his four thousand pounds.

"There're other things. Who else but Hewes could have warned Gower that I was looking for him? Wasn't that why someone tried to poison me? And take Gower himself. He's vanished too."

"All right," Jewle said. "You're trying to make things fit. Tell me some more."

"What about this, then? Hewes was going to retire: not because he was necessarily able to but because he hated the thought of living alone and scraping a living out of a third-rate agency. Gower had money and he saw a way to get it. Or it might have been that Gower was trying to blackmail him. I don't know. But it's a feasible theory and I thought you ought to hear it."

"Well—yes."

"Read through the later part of the Gower file," I said, "and see if it doesn't make sense."

He grunted.

"Read it? I know the damn thing by heart. What're you smiling at?"

"Just thinking about something that happened at Fenmarsh," I said. "We were wondering, you remember, just what might be in that grave, and I had the nerve to suggest a way to find out."

"Good God!" he said. "You're not suggesting an exhumation?"

I shrugged my shoulders.

"It's ridiculous," he said. "I'd never have the nerve to put it up. I'd be a laughing-stock."

"I know," I said. "You and Galileo."

He'd begun prowling round the room. "Even suppose you'd convinced me, which you haven't, there's too much at stake. My reputation, perhaps. I just can't do it. Not yet."

"There needn't be a conference," I said. "When you've had time to think it all over, put it up to the Commander. Confidentially. Get him worried and then sit back."

He didn't hate it, but he still didn't like it.

"Well, I'll be getting back to Broad Street," I told him. "You've let me say my piece and, honestly, I'm grateful. Now I come to think of it, it took a bit of patience to listen to me." I don't think he'd really been listening. He was still shaking his head as he helped me on with my overcoat.

The bus was taking me along the Strand towards the City. I glanced at my watch. It was getting on towards midday, and suddenly some association of ideas made me get off the bus when it stopped just short of where the old Gaiety used to be. If I'd remembered it sooner I'd have walked from the Yard to Leicester Square and gone on from there down Long Acre. Now I had to cut all the way back to the left.

There were twists and turns but I found Thurlow Street. The Three Swans was absolutely packed. I was in the saloon bar but it took me a minute to get near enough to order a drink. Two people were serving—a barman and a barmaid. Mine was the barman.

"Mr. Ranmore about?"

He gave me a queer look as he handed me my change.

"Ranmore? He died about three years ago. Didn't you know?"

"What about his daughter?"

"Oh, her," he said. "Don't know."

I gave him back the change from a pound note. "Think you could find out?"

He nodded towards the back of the bar. I took my drink and made my way towards where a woman was just getting up from a chair. I got there just in time. The crowd blocked my view of the bar, so I waited ten minutes and eased a way through again. The barman spotted me.

"Nothing doing," he said. "Not if you want to see her. She married a soldier. Last heard of she was in Cyprus. About a year ago."

I made my way out and stood for a moment by the kerb. It wasn't all that far to Tom Jordan's place. I took a few steps, then stopped. Maybe it would be as well not to get him too interested in Peplow; and if things turned out as well they might, then Peplow ought to be allowed to forget my last contact with him off Dover Street. Even if he could tell me what I wanted to know, it would be only a confirmation. Two and two make four. You don't have to write it down. You just know.

The next day I was taking an old client to lunch at the club. I set out specially early. A travel bureau wasn't much out of my way and there was something I wanted to check.

I told the clerk I was thinking of taking an immediate holiday on the French Riviera and I'd like some literature. He said if I was going by car, I might have difficulty about a ferry. I could, of course, have the car sent to Lyons or even Avignon. He was a good salesman. He gave me the details and the literature I'd asked for.

"This looks attractive," I said.

"The whole Riviera, sir, from Marseilles to Menton. If you're thinking of going at once, you'll find prices reasonable. It's still out of season."

I thanked him. I said I'd almost certainly be going. I'd get in touch with him personally if he'd give me his name.

I stayed on for a few moments at the club after my guest had left. I had a good look at those travel folders. One had a picture in colour of a girl drenching herself in sun just beyond the shadow of a gaudy beach umbrella. It was the one that dealt with the whole Riviera from

Marseilles to Menton. It was the one in which Hewes had been interested that first morning when I'd walked unexpectedly into his office.

When I got home that night I had a word with Bernice. I thought it was time we had a holiday. When I suggested the French Riviera, she was enthusiastic even though what I was thinking of was only a week. April and early May, she said, could be lovely months down there. I gambled. I said I'd get busy on it at once. With luck we could start inside a week.

At the agency we allow ourselves a three weeks' holiday, and it's quite in order to split. We weren't particularly busy and there were no difficulties. In the morning I rang my clerk and gave him the go-ahead. Any details he wanted I could let him have at once. Three days later, everything was virtually arranged. We'd be travelling by train and the car would be taken over at Avignon. It was that same afternoon that Jewle rang me.

"You busy?" he said.

"No," I said. "Unless you count packing. Bernice and I are having a holiday. Only a week. On the Riviera. We felt we needed a bit of a change."

"Perhaps you do," he said. "This was something different. I put the possibilities up to the Powers-That-Be and they're taking a chance. Tonight. Eleven o'clock. You'd like to be there? To help with identification, just in case?"

I hesitated. "I honestly don't think I would. I'll do anything else, of course, but you know what I'm like."

"That's all right," he said. "Just thought I'd let you know."

"You'll give me a ring in the morning?"

"I will," he said. "And I hope to God it's what we hope it is."

I hate exhumations. I've been at about three in my time, and for days afterwards they haunted my mind. There was the eeriness of it all: the arc-lamps, the silence, the stench of disinfectants and the contents of a coffin. Not that, before the time came that night for bed, I didn't more than once wish that I'd accepted Jewle's offer. I knew I wouldn't sleep. But I did.

The morning was almost as bad: one long fidget till Jewle rang me and, mercifully, that was not long after nine o'clock.

"You were right," he said. "Rather not tell you any more now but I'll let you have more this afternoon. All I'll say is, he wasn't in bad shape. The coffin helped. Not like that job at Fenmarsh."

It was quite late when he did ring me. I'd stayed on at the office and it was after six o'clock.

"Just got the results in," he said. "It's Gower all right. The time fits. Death from manual strangulation after a blow that slightly fractured the skull."

"What about identification?"

"Tomorrow morning. You won't be needed. Hackle and the manager at the Harringdon may be asked. By the way, when are you leaving?"

"All being well, on Monday night. We'll be back on the Tuesday week."

"I'll try and see you before you go. I'm going to be pretty busy, so, if I can't make it, give my best wishes to Bernice."

"I will," I said. "What about Hewes? You're intensifying the search?"

"You bet we are. And notifying Interpol. Can't take any chances. In case I don't see you again, mind how you go. Those French roads can be damn dangerous."

I didn't worry too much about that manual strangulation. Henry Morchard, I told myself, had been visualising something he could never really have done. Hewes was a big man, too. I remembered the huge hands that had collected those travel folders and slipped them into a drawer, and the hand that had held my own. There wasn't any doubt who'd killed Gower. And if things still went well, Jewle would never even know of the existence of a Lionel Palling.

14
JOURNEY'S END

WHEN I'd first mentioned that short holiday to Bernice, I'd had the sense to hint that there might be some combining of business with pleasure. Not that any business I might have would in any way spoil the holiday: in fact it might make it into a more attractive one. We'd once had an April in the South before and found the sea too cold for pleasant swimming, so what we might do was start at, say, Cassis and work our way leisurely along the Riviera to Menton.

Bernice loved the idea. She's quite tall and, as the French say, she watches her line, and one of the delights of that holiday would be the chance to get out of stuffy town clothes and into slim trousers and pullovers or shirts or whatever it is they're called. There's still a saving vanity in us all—not that she's as old as myself. I like to be able to stand and stare. Bernice, I suspect, likes to be stared at.

We had sleeping berths on the train that was carrying us and the car towards Avignon, and during dinner I told her a bit more about that business of mine. What I was looking for was a man. You could call him an old friend. When I admitted I had no real idea where he might be, she just couldn't believe me.

"I know," I said. "Scores of places and a few million people. But it's worth a try. Jewle wants him, so do Interpol."

"You mean he's dangerous?"

"Heavens, no," I said bravely. "He's an old friend of mine, in a way. That's why I've got something of a chance. I know him far better than they do."

He was a big man, I said: over six feet and about fourteen stone. If he spoke French at all it would be haltingly: in other words, he wouldn't be able to disguise his Englishness. In some ways he was a simple man. Anything much more than a village wouldn't appeal to him, and towns would have efficient police forces. He'd had bronchial trouble and he'd want to sit in the sun, smell the sea, gulp in good air and be left alone. He'd want to be inconspicuous and he mightn't realise that that was the very thing which might single him out. On the other hand, he'd committed what might be called the perfect crime. He'd feel himself reasonably secure.

Bernice said it was all a bit confusing. In a way it was meant to be. At any rate, we took over our car fairly early the next morning. It was a glorious day. Bernice was wearing a colourful beach suit, and before long I discarded my jacket. It's lovely country to Aix and lovelier still beyond: lonelier country with little gorges, twisting roads, straggling villages and then the long drop down to Cassis and the sea. We got there just after midday.

We'd stayed there some years before and it had changed. The season was still early but it was chock-a-block with cars. On the little square where once I'd played *boule* was a long, travelling fried-fish shop and a set of roundabouts. What should have been a happy return was suddenly something unpleasant. We didn't even stay for lunch. We bought some bread and paté and fruit and left for La Ciotat. The road runs inland and we ate the meal in the lonely heath country under some pines. I had a nap in the scented shade while Bernice read the *Petit Provençal* we'd bought in Cassis.

I'm not going to bore you with the first three days of that holiday. La Ciotat, Sanary, Bandol would be merely names unless you'd been in them. We did the little resorts south of Toulon—the mimosas were in full bloom—skirted the port and made for Hyeres. It was too large, so a check of Bormes-les-Eaux and Bormes-les-Mimosas and on through Le Lavandou. Cavaliere is only a roadside hamlet with a couple of hotels, and we had coffee there. Cavalaire is larger and we spent a night there.

Two French meals a day are too much for us so in the morning, after I'd serviced the car, we used to buy lunch for a picnic at midday. Bread is the one thing that all must eat so I'd make enquiries when I bought it. I'd describe the friend I was looking for. My French is quite good but that of my friend, I'd say, was just about enough to get by with.

Beyond Cavalaire the road turns inland, but we left it after a mile or two and took a minor road that brought us back to the sea. There're three small resorts before the same narrow road goes on to St. Tropez, and we spent best part of a day in them. Bernice loved it all. We'd brought along a couple of folding seats and she'd bought some French books. She wasn't even afraid of getting a bit tanned, and what with the beach suits, the dark glasses, the espadrilles and her dark hair, she looked as French as any.

We went on to Beauvallon and St. Maxime. The views were magnificent, especially when you turned a corner and looked down on a sheer fall to the sea and the dark blue of an inlet. And so to Val d'Esquières where we spent the night. And that's where something happened.

I was to buy *brioches* for the usual midday picnic. It was quite a small *boulangerie* and I put the usual question. There was a quick look of interest in the eyes of the elderly woman who was serving me. My friend big? He didn't speak French as well as, say, *monsieur*? Did my friend have a beard? She shrugged her shoulders when I said I didn't know.

But there was such a man. He bought bread every other day. She didn't think he was living in the town. He had been in the previous morning. His time varied but usually he came in the early morning or occasionally the late afternoon. He had first come in about three weeks ago.

It seemed promising. Bernice looked alarmed when I told her. I think she'd come privately to regard that so-called business of mine as less and less important: even as a kind of joke. What I told her was different. She began remembering things. I said we'd spend the night there and I'd be up early keeping an eye on that *boulangerie*. It might be an all-day job.

We looked round the town. There was a hotel that actually faced that *boulangerie*. There'd be plenty of time to book a room for the night, but I settled our hotel bill and drove the car down to the beach. We sat there for quite a time. Then Bernice said she didn't like spending the whole day there. Besides, we'd bought lunch so why shouldn't we drive out a little way and have the usual picnic meal.

I made for the coast road towards Boulouris and Agay. The road rose steeply, twisted and turned, fell and then rose again. You can drive for miles looking for a place for lunch and, when you do stop, you know the place you're at is worse than those you've driven by. We were lucky. We had gone about two miles and were at the very top of the rise when we saw, deep below us, one of those incredible inlets. Far down was the deep blue of the sea. The rocks ended almost at the sea's edge and there was only a yard or two of white that looked like beach. If you could ever have climbed down to it.

Fifty yards on, set back from the road on a dusty verge, was a ruined cottage, its walls plastered with advertisements. There were umbrella pines and still more lay beneath. The air was heavy with their scent and the sun hot. There was just room for the car in the scant shade of the verge. A narrow opening led by the cottage and was lost almost at once to the left. Bernice began to get lunch ready. I took the field-glasses and went through the opening. There ought to be a still better view.

I stopped dead. To the left, below the ruined cottage, the ground fell to a flat circle surrounded by the pines whose tops we had seen from the road. The soil looked hard with here and there an outcrop of rock. In that circle was a tent, its guy-ropes tied to the pines. It wasn't a bell tent. It was about ten feet by six, of dark green canvas and looking like a miniature house. The only flap that I could see was drawn.

Some twenty yards farther on where the rocks and the steep fall began there was a man. He lay in the shade of a solitary pine, his back against a rock and he seemed to be asleep. He was naked from the waist up. I put the glasses on him. He had a neatly trimmed, greying beard. But for that I'd have been certain he was Hewes.

I dodged back through the opening. Bernice had everything ready. "The man," I said, "he's out there. About fifty yards away. I've got to see him close. I think he's the one I want."

She was frightened. I smiled. "Nothing to worry about. I just want to talk to him, that's all. All I want you to do is this. We'll put everything back in the car and then I want you to watch through that opening there. Take care not to be seen. Just watch."

It was Hewes. On his feet were an old pair of *espadrilles* and the top button of his cotton trousers was undone. It was not only the beard that made him a changed man, though I'd have known him anywhere: the pasty look had gone; his chest was a warm brown and there was no wheezing in his sleep.

I had to cough twice before he stirred.

"It's you!" I said. "What in heaven's name are you doing here? Last I heard of you, you were supposed to be in Cornwall."

"Mr. Travers!" He hunted for words. "What about you, sir? What're you doing here?"

"Having a short holiday. No, don't get up. I'll sit down with you. What made you change your mind about Cornwall?"

To make it more cosy I lighted my pipe. I had to convince him I was there by chance. And I didn't want

182 | CHRISTOPHER BUSH

Bernice to be frightened. Everything had to seem nice and friendly.

"Too cold there," he said. "Here it's different."

"You been over here long?"

"Since just before Christmas. I stayed in Toulon for a bit but I don't like hotels, so soon as the weather got warmer, I started looking round. Then I found this place. I can live like a fighting-cock on a couple of pounds a week."

"You're right," I said. "All you want is a tent and a sleeping-bag. What about water?"

"There's a well up there. All I have to do is drop down a plastic bucket on a rope."

"And what do you do with yourself all day?"

"Well, I get up at daybreak. I've got a Primus so I make myself some coffee and have a bit o' breakfast. If I want anything I go down to the town. Sometimes I stop on the way back and have a swim."

"It's certainly done you good," I said. "And you never get bored?"

He actually smiled.

"Why should I? Always something to do. Also I'm studying the language. I did a little at school, so I bought a dictionary and some books. You know what I like? Sitting in a café and listening to people talk. You know: trying to make it out."

"A good way to pass the time," I waved a hand towards the rocks. "What's it like down there?"

He shook his head.

"I've only been down twice. Then I didn't like trying to get up again, so I walked round and went up the far side. It's not so steep there."

"And what about when the weather gets cold? You can't stay here then?"

"I've got it worked out," he said. "I'll store my things somewhere and move on. Italy. I might even go to Sicily. With the money I'm saving here I could afford quite a nice hotel. Then I might come back."

I'd kept him talking about himself. A faint suspicion might still be in his mind but he'd no real fear of me. The time seemed to have come to change all that.

"Aren't you forgetting one thing? What if the police catch up with you first?"

It shook him. He moistened his lips. He tried to smile.

"The police? You mean the local police?"

"Oh, no. I mean Scotland Yard and Interpol. They're looking for you. That grave at Fenmarsh was found and then they dug up the coffin at Eastgate Cemetery and found Palling."

"Palling? Who's Palling?"

He was stalling for time.

"You really want me to tell you? You mean to say you've forgotten Ranmore who kept the Three Swans near the Market? He got you to make enquiries about a man who was making up to his daughter. You found out he wasn't what he said he was. His name was Lionel Palling. He had some wealthy parents living at Sevenoaks. You'd like me to go on?"

He shifted uneasily. I thought he was going to get up but he didn't.

"All right. And what's this Palling to do with it?"

"This. You told me you never forget a face. Five years later you happened to see him going into or coming out of Hackle's office, so you followed him—just in case. When Hackle told you he was an Edward Gower who'd just collected five hundred pounds, you got into touch with this Gower at the Harringdon Hotel. He induced you to take part in a new swindle, a really big one. And why not? I think you hated that business of yours. And you knew your housekeeper hadn't long to live, so you decided it was time to look after yourself.

"I don't know who suggested what, but I know that business at the Harringdon was a fake. It was partly done to put you in the clear with Hackle and me and make it appear that Palling had gone abroad. Then you two got down to the business of blackmailing his mother. You were the Brown who telephoned her and uttered threats. I think you were the one who collected the suitcase at South Kensington Station that afternoon. You took it to Latchway Avenue. As soon as your neighbour had gone, Palling came in. You struck him down and then strangled him—"

"It's a lie. I didn't He pointed a gun at me. He wanted the lot. I gambled he wouldn't dare shoot, so I rushed him. He struck his head on the dresser but I didn't know that so I got him by the throat and shook him. That's when I saw he was dead."

"That'll be for you to explain," I said. "All I know is that you hid his body. Probably in your bedroom with the door locked. On the Friday night you made a substitution of the bodies. You'd read about some queer goings on at that ruined church at Fenmarsh and you wanted your housekeeper to have a decent burial in consecrated ground, so you took her there."

"I see." He got up on one knee. "And what're you going to do?"

"I wanted to try and find you first because I had to make a bargain with you."

He stared.

"Not what you think," I said. "It's this. You told Palling about me, and either he or you tried to get rid of me before I could make trouble. You sent me a bottle of poisoned whiskey and it was only by a miracle that I didn't drink it."

"Not me," he said. "Honest to God, Mr. Travers, I knew nothing about it. If anyone did it, it was him. You couldn't believe I'd do a thing like that."

"Let's get on with the bargain," I told him. "It's this. There's no need to drag in the name Palling. His people have suffered enough as it is. The police know nothing about that swindle you worked on his mother, so you keep it to yourself. You go on letting them know the man you killed was simply an Edward Gower and I'll keep quiet about it. That way there'll be only the one charge to face. No swindle: no attempted poisoning."

"And if I don't?"

"You can't try to blackmail me," I said, as we got to our feet. "In any case I'll have to turn you in. I'm going to stop the first car that goes by and send word to the Val d'Esquières police—"

I was a fool. I ought to have been backing away towards the road. But I wasn't. All I saw was that sudden movement of that immense fist of his. I seemed to hear a scream and then I passed out.

Bernice said I was out only about three minutes. When I came to, she had my head in her lap. I blinked. I got to my feet but my legs were weak and I was glad to rest on one knee. "What happened? Was it you I heard call out?"

"Yes," she said. "When he struck you, I screamed and I kept running towards him but he ran away. Along there."

It was incredible what she had done. I held her tightly, her cheek against mine. She was sobbing gently.

"But for you, he'd have killed me. He'd have thrown me over those rocks. He might have killed you too."

When she'd first appeared through that opening, he must have thought she was a man. That, though she didn't know it, was why he'd suddenly panicked and run. The field-glasses were where she'd dropped them. I eased her gently away and picked them up.

"Where exactly did he go?"

"Along there," she said. "I thought I heard him call out."

A little way along was a longish gap between the rocks. Maybe that was the way he'd gone down before, so I began sweeping an area with the glasses. A moment and I saw something light against the rocks about fifty feet down. I focused the glasses. It was Hewes who was lying there. He was side-faced to me, legs sprawled awkwardly. There was a dark stain across his face and he was very still.

"He's dead," I said. "He must be. No wonder you heard him call out"

She wouldn't look. All she wanted to know was what we were going to do. I said I ought to search that tent of his, but all she wanted to do was get away. I think she'd have tried to drag me if I hadn't gone.

I drove on to Agay. I found a telephone kiosk and rang the police at Val d'Esquières. I said I was a German tourist making for the Italian frontier. I described the spot where I'd pulled in off the road and seen a man lying injured on the rocks. As soon as I knew they'd understood, I rang off.

Bernice wanted to know where we were going.

"Along to Fréjus," I said. "Then we'll cut back west to Aix and Avignon. I don't think either of us wants to see that sea again."

We knew we wouldn't be hungry, but later we were. Near Aix we stopped at a little café and had coffee with that lunch we'd bought at Val d'Esquières. I owed it to her to tell her just what that morning had all been about.

We didn't get to Avignon till almost dusk. I found a hotel with garage in the Rue de la République, and the first thing I did was to send postcards to Norris, Hallows, Bertha and Jewle. I said we'd liked Avignon and the countryside so much that we'd decided to spend the whole week there instead of going south.

In the morning I bought three or four newspapers but found no reference to what I'd been hoping to see. The next morning I found it. There was only a paragraph under the heading—DEATH AMONG THE ROCKS. There was no mention of the German informant: just that the police at Val d'Esquières had found near Morny-les-Pins the dead body of an English tourist. He had apparently fallen when descending a ravine. His name was Edward Marlow. Foul play was not suspected, but the police were continuing their enquiries.

We reached home late on the Tuesday afternoon. Jewle rang soon after seven.

"Apparently you had a nice time," he said. "Bernice enjoy it, too?"

"Every minute," I said. "Couldn't have enjoyed it more."

"Well, there's one person you won't have to worry about any more—our mutual friend Hewes."

"You've caught him?"

"In a way, yes. He's dead."

"Dead! You mean in Cornwall?"

188 | CHRISTOPHER BUSH

"Oh, no. You'd never guess where. Not a hundred and fifty miles from where you were. A place called Val d'Esquières. The local police found him on some rocks leading down to a bay. He'd apparently slipped and broken his skull. He'd acquired a passport under the name of Edward Marlow. Matthews and I flew over and identified him."

"You brought his body back?"

"No point in it. Nobody was likely to claim it. He's buried in the cemetery at that Val d'Esquières place."

"And that's the end of it?"

"Just about," he said. "A little tidying up, perhaps."

I didn't see him till a fortnight later. He had some more news for me. He'd mentioned money to the Val d'Esquières police and they'd found it in a waterproof bag under a rock near where his tent had been.

"I thought they might find something," he said. "There were only a few thousand francs in his wallet and he had to have more than that. Guess how much they found."

I did some thinking "About three thousand pounds?"

He smiled. "You're miles out. Over eight thousand pounds! Practically all of it in ten-pound notes. The whole lot didn't make a bundle bigger than this. But where'd he get it from?"

"Don't know," I said. "Mind you, he was the secretive sort. And probably careful. He could have hoarded it up. A man like him could have put a lot by in sixty years."

He didn't argue the point, and I managed to turn the talk to something else. To date, he hasn't mentioned Hewes again.

One other thing happened. Morchard rang me one afternoon about a month after our return. He'd had business in the City and, since he was so close, he wondered if he might drop in on me for a minute or two. I said I'd be delighted.

He arrived in a very few minutes. Bertha brought in tea, and in the ten minutes or so of his visit, we had quite a chat. He'd been keeping well, he said, and so had his wife. She was still busy electioneering. The Fairfields were well and the children bonnier than ever. I told him about our short holiday and he said he might be going to France himself. It would depend on the Election.

When he rose to go, I asked if his worries were over. "No more looking up at that sword?"

He smiled. "Well, not very often."

"That's fine," I said.

Then I paused as if something had suddenly struck me. I frowned. He must have wondered what on earth had happened to me. Then I made a decision.

"I'd like you to assure me here and now that if I take you into my confidence you'll never mention outside the immediate family what I've decided to tell you."

"Of course," he said. "What is it?"

"Just a moment," I said. "I've got to be sure about this. I can't tell you the source of the information, but it's authoritative. If anything got out I might be in trouble."

"I assure you. I'm a man of my word."

"Then it's this," I said. "I don't think there'll be any future need for any worries at all."

"You mean . . . Lionel's dead?"

"I didn't say that," I told him. "What you read into it is for you to decide. What I do assure you is that you'll be foolish to do any more worrying."

I saw him out and he nearly crushed my hand when he left. All he could say was a goodbye and thanks. Like that listener to the Ancient Mariner, he was a man bemused.

I went back to the office. I looked at the empty cups, symbolic in a way, and did some thinking for myself. Queer thinking, in a way. It was that half-truth I'd just told Morchard that turned my thoughts to casuistry.

The casuists have argued for centuries about the lesser evil and the greater good. In our line of business a lie is merely a tool of the trade. We don't fight with clean hands. Neither do the criminals. It's a matter, as the Frenchman said, of the assassins reforming themselves first. So we lie often and we lie hard. Even a disguise is in some ways a lie. So is an obscuring of the truth.

Is then the lesser evil of a lie really for the greater good? In my younger and squeamish days I thought not. Now I'm sure it is. I don't mind if the dread Recorder hears me make that confession of faith. I'll go even farther. Maybe he'd like to look up my record and strike a new balance in his unanswerable Book.

THE END